# Dear Judy,

# What's it like at your house?

# Dear Judy, What's it like at your house?

## JUDY BAER

BETHANY HOUSE PUBLISHERS
Minneapolis, Minnesota 55438

Published by Bethany House Publishers
A Ministry of Bethany Fellowship, Inc.
6820 Auto Club Road, Minneapolis, Minnesota 55438

Printed in the United States of America

**Library of Congress Cataloging-in-Publication Data**

Baer, Judy.
    Dear Judy, what's it like at your house? / Judy Baer.
        p.  cm.

    Summary: Uses a Christian perspective to provide advice to teenage girls on how to get along with their parents and their families.

    1. Parent and teenager—United States—Juvenile literature.
2. Teenage girls—United States—Religious life—Juvenile literature.
3. Teenage girls—United States—Psychology—Juvenile literature.
[1. Teenage girls. 2. Parent and child. 3. Family life. 4. Christian life.] I. Title.
HQ799.15.B34   1992
306.874—dc20                               92–24498
ISBN 1–55661–291–5                            CIP
                                                    AC

JUDY BAER received a B.A. in English and Education from Concordia College in Moorhead, Minnesota. She has had over twenty-six novels published and is a member of the National Romance Writers of America, the Society of Children's Book Writers and the National Federation of Press Women.

Two of her novels, *Adrienne* and *Paige*, have been prizewinning bestsellers in the Bethany House SPRINGFLOWER SERIES (for girls 12–15). Both books have been awarded first place for juvenile fiction in the National Federation of Press Women's communications contest.

*I feel you, Judy Baer, are like a friend even though I have never met you.*

*—Darcy*

*I come from a family with nine kids. My sister had a baby last year, so now there are ten kids. I am twelve years old. What is your family like?*

*—Anna*

*I know this letter isn't long or official, but you sounded like I could write to you like a friend.*

*—Francine*

*I'm sorry for writing so much. It is just that I read your books and I feel that you really understand me and I can bring any problem to you!*

*—Tina*

*I don't know why I told you all this, I guess I just think of you as a friend.*

*—Sloane*

*I know you probably receive thousands (or even millions) of letters every single day, so I'm just asking that you will PLEASE write back to me.*

*—Gena*

# CONTENTS

## PART II: Siblings

Sometimes the very best gifts are the unexpected ones, those that come when your birthday is long past and it's still months until Christmas. Receiving a gift when you least expect it is one of life's nicest surprises.

I've been very lucky. I've been showered with gifts I didn't anticipate.

You see, I began writing the CEDAR RIVER DAY-DREAMS because I still remember with painful clarity my own frustrating-exciting-embarrassing-exhilarating teenage years. Also, with two daughters (now thirteen and sixteen) I'm *living* the stories I wanted to write! The bonus was the chance to develop my characters through a number of books and to see them grow and change just as "real" teenagers do.

Now, by book #18, these kids have become more real to me than some of my own relatives—after all, I spent more time with them! I've also had the opportunity to deal with some difficult issues (anorexia, suicide, alcoholism, dyslexia) to which I believe teenage girls can relate.

All that seemed exciting enough to me. I felt I'd received my birthday and Christmas gifts all wrapped up together when I signed the contract and began to write.

Books #1 and #2 were released in the fall of 1988, and

the following spring my first unexpected gifts began to arrive.

They came in the form of letters from you, my readers. There were only a few at first, then more and more, until finally the postmaster at my local post office said I couldn't have a post office box anymore. I needed to graduate to a *drawer* that would hold four times the mail! (I don't know about you, but *I* was impressed!)

Frankly, I was thrilled and honored that anyone would take the time to write to me and tell me that they enjoyed my books. And those letters held even more! They offered me an intimate look at what was on the hearts and minds of my readers.

*The problems in the books are some of the problems I have.*

—Serena

*People think I'm too young to understand the real problems of the world, but I'm very mature.*

—Virginia

*Your books are different than others because they are more like life. In other books, everything always comes out perfect and the characters all have glamorous lives. In your books, Lexi doesn't have a perfect life. No one's life is without problems and that's why other books sound so fake.*

—Andi

Exactly! Everyone has problems. In fact, so many of you have the *same* problems that I decided to create a series of books responding to the types of questions you have asked and comments you have made.

What's more, I like to think I'm *unshockable*. I don't freak easily. There are no subjects that are *taboo* with me. I'm guessing that you have realized this and feel free to share your most personal worries and fears with me. It's okay. Nothing you tell me about yourselves will make me stop caring about you.

The quotes used in this book are a combination of para-phrased questions and comments from the letters I've received. No letter has been used in its entirety. The names, ages, and details have been changed, but the situations are real. If I haven't answered a question you have, it's because no one has asked it yet.

*Do you read the letters or do your workers read them?*

—Starla

I read every letter that I receive and respond to each and every one. (I suppose, now that I've said that, I'll hear from some of you whose letters were lost in the mail or slipped through the cracks! Sorry, if that has happened.) My readers are important to me. What's more, I *like* you!

*Most big stars like you wouldn't write back to a fan. I guess you're just nice.*

—Kerry

*I can tell you care about other people. For instance, in your note at the back of your books you put, "If you feel you have any of the problems that Lexi and her friends experience, I encourage you to talk with your parents, a pastor, or a trusted adult friend. There are many people who care about you!" (I like that saying the best.)*

—Denise

*I haven't had the easiest life. I have a hard time believing people care because my dad doesn't. I've been rejected by lots of people and it's nice to know you care. Even though you've never met me or have never said directly to me that you care, I know you do. You wouldn't have put that note at the end of your books if you didn't.*

—Margaret

I *do* care. And I'm positive many other people in your life care for you as well. You must give them the chance to show you just how much . . .

*I read your book,* The Intruder, *and found it very interesting. I haven't faced a problem like that before, but if it should happen I will consult my parents or maybe you.*

—Gwen

I'm glad I'm your second choice. Kids should always go to their parents when they have problems. My books don't hold all the answers. They are just a "jumping off place" for thought and discussion.

In fact, when my publisher suggested that we title this book *What's It Like at Your House?* I was worried. After all, it's not perfect at my house. (My daughters will happily tell you that!) Still, there is one all-important element in our home. *Love.* Even when I make mistakes as a mom, my intentions are always good, not bad. My girls know that. You must believe that your own parents feel the same way.

After eighteen Cedar River Daydreams books, I've discovered that you are becoming more and more curious about *me.* You wonder what I and my family are like. Many of you ask me if I've experienced everything that's happened in the books. Happily, I can say no! I'm fortunate enough not to have experienced Alzheimer's disease, kidnapping, homelessness . . . the list goes on. But I do appreciate the fact that you'd like to know what I think about certain issues and would like to understand "who I am."

*The reason I wrote to you is because I really enjoy your books and I want to find out what your life is like.*

—Hayley

*I would like to know about your life.*

—Kendall

*I've never written to anybody important like you, except the president.*

—Tara

And here's the nicest compliment of all—

*I'd like to know if you have any kids. If so, how old are they? If you have a teenage child, he or she should feel happy to have a mother like you.*

—Ashley

*Your books have been a great inspiration to me (better than any "parent lecture" could be).*

—Becky

Well, here goes. . . .

# PART I

# Parents

● ● ● ● ● ● ● ● ●

*"My son, keep your father's commands. Don't forget
your mother's teaching. Remember their words
forever. . . ."*

PROVERBS 6:20–21

## "I Fight With My Mom/Dad..."

● ● ● ● ● ● ● ● ●

*... Does Lexi ever have a fight of any kind with her mom or dad? They are like the perfect family. Right now my mom and I can't seem to get along at all. Does Lexi ever have that kind of trouble?*

—Janelle, age 13

First of all, there are no "perfect" families. Anyone who tries to convince you that there are isn't telling the truth! After all, we're all human. Because we're human—and therefore, sinners—we can't be perfect. Just because Lexi's family—or *any* family, for that matter—*seems* like they have it all together to those looking in from the outside, it doesn't mean everything works the way it should all the time.

When you put any group of unique, diverse individuals under one roof—a family—there will be differences of opinion, disagreements, and yes, even "fights." It's *how* we handle the conflict and the arguments that's important.

As much as I'd like my own daughters to agree with me

all the time, they don't. As a mom, I can tell you it isn't always easy to accept that! Still, it is my responsibility to recognize that they are wonderful, one-of-a-kind individuals, created by God, who have their own thoughts, needs, and desires. I have to allow them to be who they are.

---

**Just because a family *appears* to have it all together doesn't mean everything works perfectly all the time.**

---

As children grow, they begin exploring their individuality (who they are as people). They start testing and improving their own decision-making skills. Painful as it might be for parents, kids even need to make some mistakes. There is no better way to learn than by the consequences of a bad decision!

For example—I learned the hard way that if I decided to leave school without permission I had to pay with some pretty high—and embarrassing—consequences. (At the time, it seemed quite logical. They were serving "mystery meat" in the lunchroom and I wanted orange soda and a candy bar. Of course, I was in second grade at the time, and not allowed to leave the school grounds!)

When I was older, I learned other, even more important things the hard way. For instance, I discovered as a seventeen-year-old that when showing off your dad's *brand-new* car was invincible, you shouldn't take it off main roads onto side streets that don't look passable. Of course, I thought I could do no wrong in this wonderful, sporty car. WRONG!

I emerged from the other side of that too-narrow side street with a scratch from one end of the car to the other. It was right through the "palomino ivory" paint (I still remember the name of the color on the brochure!) to the dark-colored body of the car. Talk about a major learning experience!

On the other hand, while my daughters are exploring more and more about who they are as individuals, I expect them to recognize the fact that I'm still "Mom." I am still responsible and accountable for their safety and well-being as well as for imparting to them morals, values, beliefs—everything they need to become reliable, dependable, trustworthy, loving, concerned adults. *Heavy duty stuff, huh?* It's no wonder families have conflict. There is a real tug-of-war going on between the job of the teenager to become independent and the job of the parent to teach, guide, nurture, and protect!

The conflict between parent and child is as old as humankind. It's not easy when you and your mom don't get along, but it is *normal.* It doesn't mean you love each other any less. It only means that you are struggling through some very difficult times and you've hit a patch of bumpy road.

That's probably where you and your mom are at right now. Hang in there. Don't give up. Things will improve with time and effort.

I do have some suggestions that might make dealing with your mom a little easier. (I'm a mom, so I think I can speak for her! Of course, I was a teenager once too. I still remember how I felt when my mother and I weren't agreeing. Frankly, those are my best credentials for writing this book!)

Everything always seems to go back to those Ten Commandments Moses collected on a mountaintop so long ago. If everyone followed *those* suggestions all the time, we wouldn't have any trouble at all!

1. "Honor your father and your mother . . ." (Exodus 20:12). What, exactly, does "honoring" your parents mean?

    Lots of things. It means showing them respect, speaking politely *to* them and even speaking nicely *about* them when they aren't around to hear it! Do you have friends who run down their parents in their conversations? Does it make you uncomfortable? It should.

    Honoring your parents means treating them the way you'd like to be treated—with courtesy, thoughtfulness, and affection. It may not always be easy to do, but it is one of God's commandments.

---

## It's not easy when you and your mom don't get along, but it is *normal.*

---

2. Try to "get into her head" and understand where she's coming from. She's no doubt looking out for your best interests. Rules and regulations are a little easier to take when you realize that they are an expression of love, not narrow-mindedness or cruelty.

3. Have patience. (I realize that when mothers speak, it's an almost automatic reaction for daughters to want to roll their eyes and say "Oh, *Mother!*") It's hard to have patience (I don't have a lot myself) but, trust me, you'll need the practice. Life will give you plenty of opportunities to use it! Besides, if your mom sees you being so "grown-up" about things, perhaps she'll settle down, too. Your relationship might improve and that's what you want most of all!

4. Express your feelings *clearly* and honestly. Mothers are not mind-readers! If you are angry because she wouldn't let you stay overnight at your friend's house, don't act as though you are angry about something else, such as having to empty the cat's litter box or clean your room. Don't show your frustration by slamming doors or saying, "You just don't *get* it!" Help her to "get it." Let her know *why* you are upset. Don't act as if the fact that she exists is the problem! Displaced anger isn't a mature way to deal with issues.

5. If *talking* things out with your mom is too difficult for you, I'd suggest *writing* out your feelings. A "Dear Mom" letter, in which you tell her how you feel, what your needs are (and, I hope, how much you love her), might break down the barriers that are building between you. My daughters have written letters to me and I cherish them.

Letters can be a window into a person's mind. Open one for your mom.

6. Remember how much she loves you. Often, when I'm saying "Stop that!" or "No, you can't go there," or "Clean your room right now!" I'm also meaning "I *love you*. It's your *behavior* that I don't like." I have a hunch your mom feels the same way.

7. Compromise. Strike a deal with your mom that will be acceptable to both of you. If she wants you to be home at ten o'clock and you ask to stay out till midnight, you'll never come to a point of compromise. But, if she's willing to let you stay out till 11:00 and you agree to call her at 10:00 to let her know you're all right, maybe you'll both feel good about the evening. Parents don't make it a goal in life to be unreasonable (although you might not believe that!). Their purpose is to raise you to safe, happy, and productive adulthood. Help them do their job. After all, you want that too, don't you?

8. Remember that troubled times pass. In a few days, weeks, or months, there will be brand-new issues troubling you, but today's spats with your mom will be history. Someday you and your mom may even be able to look back together and laugh about "that horrible year when we couldn't agree on anything." This is small comfort right now, but it might help you to put things into perspective.

Even Jesus and His parents had misunderstandings. When He was twelve, Jesus went to Jerusalem with His parents. On the way home, Mary and Joseph got their wires crossed. Each assumed that their son was with the other as they traveled in a big caravan with many other people. During the journey home, they discovered Jesus wasn't with them! *Panic city!!!* (Can you imagine what your parents would do if they discovered they'd left you behind at a rest stop while you were on vacation? Would they be upset? Disgusted? Irritated? Or furious that you hadn't made sure you'd "checked in" with one parent or the other?)

Mary and Joseph had to return to Jerusalem to find Him. It took an entire day to make the return trip. (I'll bet Joseph's blood was boiling by then. After all, he was a typical dad—worried, frightened, and angry!)

After *three days,* they found Jesus in the Temple, unconcerned about the scare He'd given them. He was listening to the teachers there and asking questions.

When His mom said, "Son, why did you do this to us? Your father and I were very worried about you. We have been looking for you" (Luke 2:48). (Can't you hear your own mom saying similar words?) Jesus couldn't see why they were upset. After all, He wasn't lost. *He* knew where He was! He was just doing His heavenly Father's work.

It's like that for teenagers sometimes. They're going about the business of being teenagers and parents just don't seem to understand. When it happens, and your parents seem particularly dense, just remember, even Jesus had your problems!

I like to think of Jesus as a teenager, a real down-to-earth kid with pumping hormones, a changing voice, maybe even skin problems. Jesus was sent to earth to experience every feeling and temptation that humans feel. That means He had moments of anger, frustration, and impatience. He, too, must have ridden that roller-coaster ride of emotions teens today feel. Take comfort in that. Your Best Friend understands. He's been there.

*My problem: My dad thinks he owns the world. My mother is a little too bossy. Me, my mother, and my father get into fights during the day for who-knows-what. We get into fights at night because I stay up too late reading.*

—Abbie, age 10

Dads can be like that. So can moms. So can kids, for that matter. Sounds to me like you're chafing under too many rules and instructions right now. You're stretching your mental muscles, looking for a little extra freedom, and your parents are getting on your nerves.

That's all right. I get on my kids' nerves occasionally, too. It happens to everyone. They've always felt free to tell me when I'm driving them a little bit crazy. I can accept that. I just smile and say, "I'm a mom. It's my job."

Attempt to listen to and understand *their* point of view. Once you understand your parents and their passionate love for you, it may be easier for you to accept what they have to say.

If you're getting into fights and can't even remember what the fights were about, then they certainly weren't worth having! I'm a big believer in what I call "picking my battles." That means I refuse to bicker over little, unimportant things. If something is so important to me that it's worth disagreeing about with another person, then that issue must be very special to me.

When you see or feel a "fight" coming on, ask yourself if the issue is really worth getting all upset about. If it's not, *choose not to fight!* If it is important to you to read at night, either go to bed a little earlier or negotiate a different bedtime.

---

### Pick your battles carefully. Refuse to bicker over trivial, unimportant things.

---

I like that word *negotiate*. It means to work out an agreement that is satisfactory to both you and your parents. They might be happy to let you read in bed if you'd arrange a "lights out" time in advance. If you wait until the last moment to plead for more time, when the scolding has already started and you're getting angry, you'll all be miserable.

As a Christian, you have a responsibility to respect and obey your parents. You should show this respect even if you think your parents are asking too much.

I didn't say this would be easy, but it's definitely worth a try. I believe that God will reward your efforts. After all, He wants your home to be happy and full of harmony, too.

*I guess you could say that my life has been pretty screwed up. I am fifteen years old and I am living at a group home. My mother and I haven't been getting along, so I chose to move here for six months.*

—Brita, age 15

I congratulate you on trying to get your life back together! It's not easy. In your case it means separation and heartache, but *don't give up!* Your life was not "screwed up" overnight, and the damage can't be undone quickly, either.

Take your life at the group home one day at a time. Live that day to its fullest. Learn all you can. Enjoy what there is to enjoy. In six months you can be an entirely different person than you are today. Look ahead with optimism. Go for it!

And remember, God will always be there for you. If He feels far away right now, it's because during the turmoil in your life, *you've* stepped away from Him. He wants you back. You are precious to Him.

## For Others Whose Families Are in Trouble:

Sometimes things *really* go wrong in a family. When this happens, kids and parents can't deal with it on their own. That's when someone outside the family unit needs to step in to help get the family back on track again.

This is the point at which counselors, pastors, therapists, and social workers are so important. *A child or family in trouble should get help!* There are professionals who are trained to deal with every situation. I encourage anyone who needs professional help to seek it.

If *finding* help seems like a huge and overwhelming task, here is a list of places to turn to for professional help:

1. The pastor of your church. (If he doesn't feel competent to help you, he can give you the name of someone who is.)
2. Your school counselor (or if there is no counselor, a favorite teacher).

3. A trusted and respected older friend or family member. (Remember, however, that just because someone is an adult doesn't mean that he or she is always a good counselor. If you get advice that feels or sounds wrong to you, go to someone else. Adults have differing amounts of common sense, just as younger people do. Not all adults are equally wise or experienced, either. That still leaves you with the responsibility of deciding who is giving you the best advice.)
4. A social worker.

There are other people you could turn to as well, but these are probably the easiest to reach. It's not a crime to ask for help if you need it. It is a crime *not* to!

Never be ashamed to ask for help. Being too proud to get whatever assistance you need will only hurt you. You do not need to be alone with your problems. There are others who care and can help you if you seek them out.

*You are not alone.*

## "I'm Lonely"

● ● ● ● ● ● ● ●

*There are many times that I wish I had Lexi's family. They are so loving. And it seems they are that way most of the time. I don't have a family like that. I am there, but no one really notices. I guess we can never have all the things we want in life.*

—Andrea, age 12

*My dad is gone all the time. My brother died, so I am alone most of the time.*

—Heidi, age 14

Your letters make my heart ache. I wish that everyone could go through life without having to experience the disappointment and despair that your letters express.

Loneliness is one of the most painful, esteem-depleting emotions there is. When a person is lonely, everything else seems wrong too. It colors your entire life an ugly, depressing gray. You look around and see that everyone else's life appears complete and happy. Then you start to ask, "Why me? Why does everything go wrong for me?"

---

**Sometimes the best cure for loneliness is to look around for someone to whom *you* can be a friend.**

---

As I've said before, there are no perfect lives or perfect families. Because you are closest to your own family, you are able to see the flaws in it. It's harder to see the imperfections in the lives of others, but they are there. Trust me, other people with smiles on their faces are hurting inside too.

God speaks to loneliness many times in the Bible. He even had to reassure His own worried disciples that when He went to Heaven to be with His Father, they would not be left alone! He said, "I will not leave you all alone like orphans. I will come back to you" (John 14:18).

Jesus meant that even though he would no longer be with them physically, He would send His Holy Spirit to live in the minds and hearts of those who believed in Him. That means that even though we can't see or touch Jesus, we can sense His presence and hear His voice in our minds.

That might seem like pretty small comfort when your father isn't home, your parents don't seem to know you're there, or there's no one to talk to when you need somebody desperately, but give God a chance. He even left instructions in the Bible on how to do it. "Call to the Lord, and the Lord will answer you. You will cry out to the Lord, and he will say, 'Here I am' " (Isaiah 58:9).

In Cedar River Daydreams #17, *The Lonely Girl,* Angela Hardy felt alone and unaccepted by her peers. As crazy as this may sound, Angela actually created some of her own loneliness! Afraid of being shunned, she isolated herself from people—like Lexi and Egg—who wanted to be her friends.

Sometimes, as a sort of protection, we build walls around ourselves that, in the end, only increase our unhappiness. The cure? Look around for someone to whom *you* can reach out, and demolish two cases of loneliness by being a friend.

Remember, as a Christian, you have a built-in Best Friend, one you can always talk to. One who will always listen.

Although that's great news, there's more to this loneliness stuff, especially where your parents are concerned. *Please tell them how you feel!* They may be so busy trying to make a good life for you (by earning money, cooking meals, doing laundry, etc.) that they've forgotten the importance of just being together, of laughing, talking, or playing a game.

That can happen to even the best parents. We tend to forget that our kids will remember the times we shared together long after they've forgotten that we got the laundry done! I don't want my kids to brag to their friends that "Mom keeps a clean house." I'd rather they say, "She always has time for me." If your parents had a choice, they'd want the same.

Remind your parents that you love them and want to spend time with them. Share your feelings and give them the opportunity to help you with your loneliness.

*My father has been gone for almost a month and I've only talked to him once. I'm failing every class in school except physical education. Everything has been going wrong this year. My parents are broke. My dad's never around. Our car keeps breaking down. My best friend just moved away.*

—Debra, age 13

When one thing goes wrong, doesn't it seem as though *everything* goes wrong? It's that old "domino theory"— touch the first domino in the line and all the other dominos fall down too. That's what's happening to you. If your dad didn't need work, he wouldn't have to be away. If you weren't short of money, you could get the car fixed. If you didn't have all these other problems, you could concentrate at school. Am I right?

Many of the things that are happening in your life, you

can't change. I'd suggest that you pick the one or two things you can control and work on them. You can't do anything about your dad's business, the car, or the fact that your friend's family moved away. You can, however, get a grip on yourself and concentrate on schoolwork. You can also make an effort to make some new friends. Pulling up your grades and finding someone new to hang out with might not fix everything, but it will make you feel better about yourself and your life.

I've had times when I don't feel as though I'm in charge of anything in my life. It all seems to be spinning out of control. Do you know what I do then? I clean a closet! It sounds crazy, but it feels good to have at least one little thing that isn't a disaster. Take control of what you can. Trust your parents to help as much as they can. Turn the rest over to that Best Friend.

## THREE

## "My Parents Don't Pay Any Attention to Me..."

● ● ● ● ● ● ● ● ●

*My parents don't pay attention to me, but when they do, they yell at me.*

—Dawn, age 12

The biggest problem in your letter is the statement, "My parents don't pay attention to me . . ."

If I were to guess, from that one statement, what is going on at your house, I would say that your parents are very busy—too busy—making a living, cleaning, cooking, working, working, working, to realize what effect it's having on you. People who are too busy often have short fuses and blow up easily. I'd guess that your parents think that providing food, clothing, and shelter is their job. They may have temporarily forgotten that there's not only a physical side to raising a family but also emotional and spiritual sides as well.

Your family needs to improve their lines of communication. Why don't you be the one to start? Try to find a time when your parents are not so busy or harried and talk to them. Tell them (one at a time or together) that you love them and would like to spend more time with them. Explain that you are lonely for their company. Or suggest, "Mom, could we go shopping together? I'll help you buy groceries. Maybe we could go out for ice cream afterward."

---

### Try to view your mother or father as a potential friend
### —you might discover that he or she makes a good one!

---

If this sort of gentle nudging doesn't do the trick, perhaps you should talk to another adult you trust and who knows your family well (a pastor, aunt, or teacher, perhaps). Someone near to you might see more clearly what is happening in your family and be able to give you advice and direction.

## FOUR

## "My Parents Are Divorced ..."

● ● ● ● ● ● ● ● ●

*What does the Bible say about divorce? What are your views? My parents are in the middle of a divorce now.*

—Kirsten, age 15

*No one* likes divorce. When two people marry, they always want it to be for life. Therefore, when it's not, everyone is hurt, disappointed, and unhappy.

The one thing you have to remember when your parents divorce is that *it's not your fault!* Children often mistakenly blame themselves for the things that happen in their parents' lives, but divorce is something for which parents must take *full* responsibility. So, if you've got any feelings of guilt or ideas that if you'd behaved differently your parents might have stayed together, forget it. You didn't cause the divorce and you alone can't fix your parents' lives. Your only job is to love your parents as you always have.

Divorce is mentioned often in the Bible and is not encouraged. God's heart grieves at the pain inflicted upon the family of divorce. "God has joined the two people together. So no one should separate them" (Mark 10:9).

Despite these statements, there is also a wonderful story in John 4 that tells of Jesus' forgiving attitude. Jesus came to a well in Samaria and sat down beside it to rest. While He was there, a Samaritan woman came to draw water from the well. She came at noon, the hottest time of the day, because she wanted to be alone. You see, she'd been divorced not once, but *five* times, and others tried to avoid her. She was an outcast because of her many divorces.

Even though the Jews (Jesus was a Jew) and the Samaritans didn't get along and the woman had been divorced many times, Jesus *still* asked her to draw water for Him from the well. He had many good excuses to avoid such a woman, yet *He didn't.*

What does that tell us? Though the Bible doesn't approve of divorce, Jesus forgave the woman for her past. Even though Jews didn't like to use things that Samaritans had used, He asked her to draw Him some water to drink. That would be like sharing your lunch with the person you least liked in the lunchroom at school! Jesus chose to forgive her, to love her, and to not hold her past against her.

That's the good news in the Bible. Even though we might make bad choices or do things we shouldn't, we have a God who is able to forgive us and help us start over.

So then, what does the Bible say about divorce? It's not God's plan. Marriage is meant to be a lifelong commitment between two people. But when things *do* go wrong, we have a loving, forgiving Father to turn to for help. That's better than good news. That's *great* news!

If you are feeling really helpless about this divorce, there is one thing you can do. You can pray for your parents. Remember that Best Friend I keep talking about? Ask Him for help. Sometimes praying doesn't seem to help right away or at all, but don't worry about that. God works on hearts and minds as well as bodies. He works in ways that can't always be seen immediately. Perhaps your parents will stay divorced even though you pray desperately that they get back together. That doesn't mean your prayer has failed. It might mean that God is working on their minds, helping them to be civil and courteous to each other. Or it could be that God will work on *your* mind, helping you to accept what has happened.

---

**God meant marriage to be a lifelong commitment between two people. But when things *do* go wrong, we have a loving, forgiving Father to turn to for help.**

---

It doesn't matter that we don't always understand how God works. All we need to know is that He's always working for our best interest. Once you turn it over to God, try not to worry anymore. Worry only gives people stomachaches and frown lines. It's not good for much else, so get rid of it.

*The parents of one of my friends have separated. She's having a hard time dealing with it. She says nobody loves her or cares what happens to her. She says the only reason her mom keeps her is so she can get money from her dad. She's very confused and she is having a rough time. What should I say? I'd really like to help her but I'm not sure where to begin.*

—Maggie, age 13

Your friend sounds hurt and bitter. That's perfectly normal. Even though she feels awful, her experience is one lots of people have had. Not much comfort right now, huh?

One thing she must do is *talk to her parents.* They are the ones who can assure her that people *do* love her and care what happens to her. It is no wonder she's confused. The two people she loves most are acting as though they hate each other. She feels like a weapon in a nasty game between them. It's important that she get her feelings out in the open. The sooner this happens, the sooner she can begin to recover and adapt to her new family situation. Your friend no doubt wants her family to be the way it used to be. She feels abandoned, rejected, and neglected by her parents. Unfortunately, her parents are having their own problems and probably aren't tuned in to her feelings right now. They don't have the emotional energy left over to help their daughter.

It is not surprising this family is in trouble.

A divorce or separation is very much like having a death in the family. A precious relationship is lost. Sometimes people need time to grieve. Crying is okay. She's experiencing something worth crying about.

The very best thing for this family right now would be counseling. They all have lots of problems to work through. Even if her parents refuse to go, counseling would be good for your friend. Start with a school counselor or a pastor. Tell her to ask for help. There's no shame in that. Having an adult to talk to will help your friend to realize that although her life will change, it won't be over. With time will come happier days and the ability to accept her parents' separation or divorce. It will be tough, but it can be done.

*My mom and her boyfriend, Kevin, are getting married. It will be my mom's third marriage. I haven't heard from or seen my second dad for two years. I do see my real father. He is a salesman. He has been to six states already this fall.*

*—Anne, age 12*

Sometimes families get so mixed up and "blended" that it's hard to keep them straight. Your mother's marriages and divorces are something you cannot control. It's a helpless feeling to see people you've learned to love exit from your life. That is the case with your second dad. When he left your mom's life, he chose to leave yours as well. Children *want* two parents. They also want their lives to be free of turmoil and change, but that doesn't always happen. Divorces are sometimes so bitter or unfriendly that the man and woman involved don't want anything to do with each other when it's all over. Two people who once loved each other are no longer even friends. That's tough to accept, but *always remember that it's not your fault.*

It's good that you have kept in touch with your natural

father. He obviously cares for you despite his divorce from your mom. Enjoy your time with him.

*My mom is a single parent, so I try to help her out a lot.*
—Carla, age 17

Good for you! You sound like a girl who's been through the pain and trauma of a divorce and has come out on the other side stronger and wiser!

Have you heard of "tempered steel?" To make steel as strong as it can be, it is subjected to very high heat. It would seem that those searing temperatures would melt the steel. Instead, it comes out even tougher and stronger than before!

A divorce in your family can be a little like that. It is an experience that seems so horrible that you are afraid it will crush you. But, if you learn what you can from it and grow through it, the experience will make you more compassionate and mature than before.

What can you learn from a divorce? That depends. Each situation is different. Maybe what you'll learn most is about yourself. You might discover that you are able to take some of the responsibility for chores off your parents' shoulders. You might find that you won't shrivel up and die when your parents separate, but that you are stronger and more mature than you first realized. It isn't easy or fun, but it's something in your life you'll need to get through. What you can't control, you still must manage.

---

### Allow the crises in your life to help you grow into a stronger, more compassionate human being.

---

Everyone has trouble in their lives. Since you can't make those problems go away, you might as well turn them around and use them to grow, change, and make yourself an even better person.

I shouldn't assume, however, that just because your

mom is a single parent that she's been divorced. Perhaps she's widowed or has never been married. Families come in many configurations. Each family has its own special needs.

If your dad has died and your mom is widowed, your situation can be especially painful. You and your mom need each other more than ever. It's good that you are there for her.

Children of one-parent families often have to grow up quickly and take on more responsibility at an earlier age. That's tough, but it doesn't have to be all negative.

"When life gives you lemons, make lemonade." There is a lot of wisdom in that popular comment. You can turn this sour situation into something useful, or you can let it make you bitter and unpleasant. If you can face any problem with optimism and hope, it will seem easier. It's really your choice.

Sound tough? It is. But you have a loving heavenly Father to help you through it all. With time and patience, and God on your side, you can come through this situation as strong as tempered steel.

*Your books encourage me to keep walking with God through my problems with my grandfather and my parents. My parents are divorced and both remarried, and my grandfather is an alcoholic. My mother is under a lot of pressure from all the trouble my grandfather is giving. My brothers and I put up with my dad.*

—Amy, age 9

You've got an entire handful of difficult circumstances to deal with! In a situation like yours, I'd recommend that you talk to a counselor or pastor about all that is going on in your life. He or she won't be able to "fix" any of it (your grandfather will still be an alcoholic, your parents divorced, etc.), but they will be able to give you tips about handling your own feelings and emotions in a healthy manner.

People from very bad circumstances can become wonderfully compassionate, caring individuals. But in order for that to happen, you must keep yourself healthy—mentally, physically, and spiritually. There's an organization for alcoholics called Alcoholics Anonymous. Alateen is a group within this organization for the people who have to live with alcoholics. It might be a very good idea for you and your mother and brothers to look into this organization. It can help you cope with your grandfather. Just because you can't change *him* for the better doesn't mean you can't change *yourself*!

## FIVE

# "Who Should I Live With?"

● ● ● ● ● ● ● ● ●

*You do such a great job solving Lexi's and her friends' problems that I was hoping you could help me with one of mine.*

*My mom and dad got divorced four years ago. I have been living with my mom. My dad wants me to come and live with him. I can't say no, but I can't say yes, either, because I don't know if I can leave my mom. What should I do?*

—Candy, age 13

You're in a tough spot, because you care deeply for both your parents, and now you have a very difficult decision to make. It sounds as if there are both good and bad things about either decision. I'd recommend that you explain your feelings to each of your parents just as you have explained them to me. Obviously, they both love you very much and don't want you to be confused or unhappy. You must be honest with them, however, and tell them how you feel. Ask them to put their differences aside and help you to decide what to do.

If one of your parents has legal custody of you, then

the decision has been taken out of your hands. If this is the case, make it a goal to try to be content wherever you are. Since you can't change your circumstances, you might as well try to be happy in them.

If the decision has been left in your hands, your first priority should be to pray for help to make the right decision. God knows what's best for you. He's the wisest One of all, so get His input on this situation.

Then whatever decision you make, *enjoy.* Don't feel guilty. You can't be in two places at once, so, once your decision is made, make the best of it. If you keep on wondering if you made a mistake, and look backward instead of forward, you'll be miserable and unhappy with whichever place you have chosen to live.

## SIX

# "I've Got a Stepparent..."

● ● ● ● ● ● ● ● ●

*Our family has been through a lot of trials. It has not been easy to accept strangers (my stepfather and his children) into our home. What has happened is a lot like your book,* The Intruder, *while Amanda lived in the Leighton home as a foster child. I haven't made it easy for my stepfather and his kids. I have been "right down" selfish.*

*I used to have my mother to myself. I had an easy life until my mom got remarried. Then my whole life caved in.*

—Deidre, age 13

It's not easy to accept a stepparent into the family. I wouldn't like it either, at least not at first. After all, you'd rather have your "real" mom or dad than this "stand-in." However, it's better to face reality as soon as possible and get down to the business of dealing with this new parent because he is now a part of your life—whether you like it or not. Life will be much easier at your house and for you if you can accept this fact.

You'll have to learn, just as Lexi did in *The Intruder,* to give this new person a chance. Meet him halfway. Don't go out of your way to make trouble for him. This may be hard—especially if you feel resentment toward this stranger who has entered your life and taken over so much of your mother's time.

It's understandable that you want your own two parents to be together. Every child does! Remarriage is a sure sign that your mom and dad won't get back together. No wonder you resent the new person in the family! He represents the end of a happy, familiar way of life and the beginning of a new, unknown one. What's more, your new stepfather and family may have rules and habits that seem strange and foreign to you. It's frightening to think of life being so unalterably changed. It's hard not to be angry with everyone involved. After all, you didn't give them permission to mess up your life, too!

But what's done is done. Now you have a new stepparent. What's next?

My own children, as little girls, had a strong sense of who did and did not have authority over them. Occasionally we would leave them with babysitters who, for one reason or another, rubbed the girls the wrong way. When the sitter tried to correct or discipline the girls, my children would respond by saying, "But you're not the boss of me! My mom and dad are the boss of me!"

That's pretty much what you're saying right now. You don't feel your new stepfather is "the boss of you."

---

**Always remember that good things *can* come from bad situations—never lose hope or give up trying.**

---

It's *hard* to take orders from that new parent. What right does he have telling you what to do? He's not your *real* dad. He'd just better stay out of your way and out of your life—right?

Wrong.

Your new stepparent has a big interest in seeing your family run smoothly. After all, he loves your mom and wants to stay with her forever. The last thing they need is a crabby kid trying to blow up all the fences they are mending.

You want your mom happy, right? If she's happy, you're happier too. Even if you resent this new person in your life, be practical. It's easier to live in a happy home than a sad one. Approach it from that angle. Make your goals: (1) acceptance of your new family, and (2) a peaceful household. You might be surprised that eventually you'll begin to enjoy that new person in your life. You might even see something of what your mom saw in him (his sense of humor, compassion, intelligence, whatever) when she fell in love!

This new dad might seem to be doing everything in his power to sabotage your best efforts at peacemaking. He might lay down his own rules in your house. Don't immediately decide to rebel. Understand that he's trying to make sense and order out of his new situation, too. It takes time to build friendship and respect. Hard as it might be, give him some time to prove himself and hope he does the same for you.

If you *do* discover yourself beginning to actually *like* this new stepparent, don't panic! You aren't being disloyal to your "real" dad. He doesn't want you to be miserable either. It will be a big relief to him to see you settling in to a peaceful family life.

Perhaps, if everyone tries to build and maintain healthy, loving relationships, you'll find yourself with not two, but three (or even four) parents who care deeply about you. Good things can come from bad situations—don't ever lose hope or give up trying.

(About those stepchildren of his—I'll cover that under the siblings section. That's an entirely different ball game!)

*I have this problem with my stepdad. My mom let me date when we were in North Carolina, but now I have to wait until I'm sixteen. It's not that bad. It's only a year away. But the thing is, he doesn't trust me. And that really ticks me off because he hardly knows me. And when I ask to go somewhere I get yelled at. But when I don't have anywhere to go, they yell at me to do something useful with my time. I don't know what to do anymore. I can't talk to anyone about my problems—especially my parents. I've tried to talk to my school counselor but that only helps for a while. If you could, please help me and give me some advice.*

—Georgina, age 15

Maybe the reason he doesn't trust you is *because* he doesn't know you!

Perhaps he's nervous about having a teenager (some people are, you know). He might have read too many newspaper accounts or seen too many TV shows about rebellious teens. Maybe he thinks that if he doesn't "come down hard" at first you'll get out of hand. He didn't raise you from babyhood, so he really doesn't know much about you (or what a nice person you really are). *So show him!*

Can you think of something that the two of you might do together? If he's a golfer, ask him to teach you the fundamentals of the game. If he plays softball, maybe you can entice him into a game of catch. When you have a question about something, try going to him first (parents love trying to help).

It's good that you've talked to your counselor. Keep on doing that. It's a safety valve so you don't explode with all the frustration you're feeling right now. And this *will* take time. You and your stepdad have to build a mutual trust and respect between you. That's a slow process, but definitely worth the effort. Hang in there (and read the next statement. . . . )

*The only person who really cares about my feelings is my stepdad. I really like him.*

—Joan, age 11

Stepdads *can* be the greatest thing since chocolate! And how fortunate you are to have a good one. Here's a suggestion—be sure to *tell* him how much you appreciate him. Everyone likes a compliment now and then. How wonderful it would be to hear that from a stepdaughter!

(One more thing—I doubt that your stepdad is the only person who really cares about your feelings. Evidently he is the best at showing you how he feels, however. If this troubles you, talk to your stepdad. Ask him to help you through your feelings.)

---

**School counselors and pastors provide a safe place for us to vent the frustrations we may be feeling during a crisis.**

---

## SEVEN

## "I Fight With My Stepmother..."

● ● ● ● ● ● ● ●

*My stepmother is beginning to bother me. She's a nice Christian woman. My older sister gets along with her just fine, but I can't help but argue and stuff like that. Even my thoughts are nasty. This is beginning to scare me a little bit because I've never felt this way before. Even my personality has changed. My thoughts are altogether rotten. I'm beginning to think and do stuff I never have done before.*

—Leah, age 16

Just because bad thoughts come into your head doesn't necessarily mean you've sinned. Lots of thoughts go through a person's head in a day. You can be sure that we aren't proud of all of them. It's what you *do* with those thoughts that counts.

Do you *enjoy* those bad thoughts? Do you roll them around in your mind and expand upon them? Once a nasty thought enters your mind, do you relish it, or do you push it out and try to fill that space in your mind with something more pleasant and positive?

Martin Luther said, "We can't stop the birds from flying over our heads, but we can stop them from building nests in our hair." Our bad thoughts are like birds whizzing by. You can't help that they are there, but you *can* chase them away and not feed and water them!

When the bad thoughts come, try to replace them with good thoughts. Do you have any Christian music that you really like? Turn it on. "Think about the things that are good and worthy of praise. Think about the things that are true and honorable and right and pure and beautiful and respected" (Philippians 4:8).

Do you play the piano? Start playing! Do you like to read or bake? Grab a book, or a bowl and spoon!

"Okay, fine," you say, "but what if that doesn't work?"

Then it's probably time to talk to someone about your feelings. I'd recommend asking your pastor to find the time to talk with you. You obviously don't want to feel resentful or negative about your stepmother. With some counseling, your pastor should be able to determine why these negative thoughts have popped up just recently and give you some ideas about controlling them.

*Once my stepmom called me a slut. I feel really hurt about that.*

—Meredith, age 11

I'd feel hurt too. But since that word has slipped out of your stepmother's mouth and is already floating around in your brain, what are you going to do about it?

There are a couple of choices: (1) You can stay mad at her forever (and forever is a long, long time), or (2) you can *forgive* her. I'd go with the second choice if I were you. If you hang on to your anger and hurt, it will only do you more harm. You'll carry that ugly word around in your head and heart, watching and waiting for the next time she says something inappropriate. Who wants that for a hobby? Not you!

As my sixteen-year-old read through this manuscript, she took issue with my response to this statement. "You know, Mom," she said, "sometimes kids deserve what they get from their parents. Don't you think kids have to be responsible for their actions, too? What if she really did something wrong?"

That made me stop and think. As a parent, I consider the word "slut" much too harsh a term to be used when talking to an eleven-year-old. But, as my daughter suggested, when there's trouble in a family, *everyone* has to ask themselves in what way they've contributed to the problem.

Was that mother's harsh response appropriate? No. Was her anger justified? I don't know. Only the people involved know that. When trouble explodes, it's a good idea to step back and ask yourself if you are in some way responsible. If you know you are, make some changes. If you know the anger was unjustified, then listen to the advice in Ephesians 4:31–32: "Do not be bitter or angry or mad. Never shout angrily or say things to hurt others. Never do anything evil. Be kind and loving to each other. *Forgive each other just as God forgave you in Christ.*"

The reason we can forgive others is because God forgave us for so many things in our own lives. As human beings we've really blown it. We've said and done about a zillion crummy things and yet *God is still able to forgive us*! That's why we should forgive others.

Let God take care of injustices. Don't answer one harsh word with another. Continue to be the nicest you can be. Some days that might be hard, but give it a try. At least you'll be happy about yourself.

---

**When trouble erupts, ask yourself, "Am I responsible in any way?"**

## EIGHT

---

# "My Dad Had an Affair..."

**● ● ● ● ● ● ● ● ●**

*I found out about a month ago that my dad had an affair with a lady while he was still married to my mom! I can't believe that my caring dad would do that! I feel shaky when I talk about it.*

—Nora, age 11

*My parents have been fighting a lot lately. My father moved out and is seeing another woman. Please send me a book by you to help me to understand what other people are going through today.*

—Desiree, age 11

Your parents have temporarily (at least I hope it's temporary) fallen *out* of love. They've lost or forgotten the feelings they once had for each other and have begun to drift apart.

This is a bad situation for a married couple because it sets up a scenario Satan loves to see. It is a situation in which a husband or wife is apt to be tempted to be unfaithful. Just as much as Satan loves to see someone fall into this trap, God hates it.

In fact, in the New Testament, adultery is the *only* reason two people were allowed to get a divorce. The Bible is stern about such things because this sin can hurt so many people—innocent people, like you.

It's not surprising that your mom and dad are fighting. They have big issues to work out. It sounds as though they aren't doing a very good job of it—yet. Hopefully they will realize that they need help to get through a time like this. There are professional counselors, therapists, and pastors who can guide them through the maze of hurt and pain and put them back on the right path.

You'll need help, too. It's scary to see the people you love and depend upon most in the entire world fighting, crying, and losing control. It makes you feel as though your entire life is blowing up in your face and you can't do a thing to stop it. Keeping your worries inside won't help. They'll just get bigger and more unmanageable. Talk them out instead. Perhaps there's a teacher or adult friend you can talk to about your fears.

I encourage my own daughters to keep a journal. When you have feelings, fears, and emotions that need to come out, write them down. It's strange, but the very act of writing things out sometimes helps to put problems in perspective. It's as if by putting your problems onto paper, you remove them from the center stage of your mind. What seems huge and unmanageable in your imagination may seem smaller and more manageable on paper. If nothing else, it is a way to vent your feelings rather than store them inside until you want to burst.

My own daughter has told me that writing down her problems puts things in perspective for her. Gigantic problems that seemed nearly insurmountable when she recorded them in her journal seem manageable and even unimportant when she looks back on them weeks later. Your problems aren't minor, but you'll need every bit of help you can get to assist you through this troubling time. If journaling helps, do it.

---

## Keep a journal. Writing out your thoughts and concerns helps to put them into perspective.

---

There are several things you must remember about your dad's affair. First of all, you can't control his actions. You can't stop him from seeing this other woman until *he* wants to stop. Don't feel responsible in any way for what he is doing. It has nothing to do with you. Many times children blame themselves for what happens in their parents' lives. Please believe me, *this is not your fault!*

Secondly, understand that it is normal and natural to be angry with your dad for doing this to you and your mother. But don't stop there! Harboring anger is unhealthy for you. It only makes you feel small and shriveled up inside. Therefore, even though you may be very angry with your dad, it is important for your own well-being that you forgive him.

"But that's too hard!" you say? It *is* hard! Sometimes it feels right and good to hang on to anger. Still, the Bible says, "When you are praying, and you remember that you are angry with another person about something, then forgive him. If you do this, then your Father in heaven will also forgive your sins" (Mark 11:25).

The Bible says a lot about forgiveness. If it is hard for you to forgive your dad for what he's done, you can then see what a big and wonderful gift it was for God to forgive *all* of us for our sins when Jesus died on the Cross! That's some kind of love, isn't it? That love, so much love that Someone *died* for you, should give you hope and comfort right now.

Still tempted to "show" your dad what a rotten thing you think he did? Then listen to Proverbs 20:22—"Don't say, 'I'll pay you back for the evil you did.' Wait for the Lord. He will make things right."

Leave it in God's hands.

What a great idea! Turn all those fears and emotions over to Him. Let Him do the worrying for you. Let Him help you to understand the confusing world of adults and the bad choices they sometimes make. You've got a Friend to help you through all of this. Let Him.

If you can get past the feelings of betrayal and loss, you can once again enjoy the relationship with your dad you were afraid you had lost. And that's what you fear most, isn't it? Losing your dad? The idea that he might not love you anymore? It's scary. It's hard. It's crummy. But you'll make it.

*My dad had an affair. I've accepted it but my mother hasn't. It was hard because I've always been "Daddy's Little Girl." That made me want to ask God, "Why me?" My dad is not a Christian. When I visit him, life is a lot different.*

—Laura, age 13

"Why me?" Isn't that the question we always ask when something goes really wrong? "Why couldn't this rotten thing happen to someone else?"

You feel betrayed. But now that it's happened, what next? Right now, when you need support and encouragement from your mom, she probably hasn't got the emotional strength to give it to you. She's still feeling shocked, hurt, and depressed.

Though I feel like I'm repeating myself, I have to say this again and again because it's so true—you and your mom need professional help. A family counselor can help you with your questions—and believe me, you've asked a big one.

The second issue you are struggling with is your father's rejection of your beliefs. That's rough too. As with the divorce, you have little control over what your father does or thinks. You do, however, have Somebody on your side who can make all the difference.

You have the greatest source of power in the universe— God—to tap into for your own strength and faith. He can also work on your dad's heart. Ask Him. Then trust that He has heard your prayer and will answer in His own time and way.

The other thing you have going for you is the fact that

you are a Christian. You can show your dad by your attitude, demeanor, and actions that you have something very special in your life—God. That's what witnessing is all about—showing others through your behavior that you are a new creation, different than you were before because of what God has done in your life. "If anyone belongs to Christ, then he is made new. The old things have gone; everything is made new!" (2 Corinthians 5:17).

That's really all you can do, because, after all, you cannot control another person, only yourself. But, with God on your team, who knows what victories you might win?

## NINE

## "I'm Curious About My Father..."

● ● ● ● ● ● ● ● ●

*My parents were divorced when I was born. I have never seen my father. Sometimes I dream about him and wish that I could see him, but who wouldn't? I know, compared to some, I got off very lucky not having to go through the hurt of their divorce. People sometimes say they're sorry for me, but I have learned to accept it. It is still hard for Mom to talk about the divorce.*

—Crystal, age 12

You've got the same problem that adopted children encounter. There's a faceless person out there somewhere who gave you life. It's more than curiosity that compels you to wonder about your father. There are dozens of questions surrounding this man that you have not had satisfactorily answered.

Your feelings are perfectly natural. Anyone would wonder about a father they had never seen. What's more, someday, it's only fair that you get some answers.

It sounds as though your mom is still hurting. She obviously wants to close that chapter of her life and not look back. I can understand that. I might also feel that way in her situation. But that leaves you feeling very up in the air and unsettled. You have questions that need to be addressed. Once you have some answers, then you can quit looking backward and look to the future instead.

Someday, when the time feels right, you might want to tell your mother about your questions. Explain that it's important to you to settle your past and get on with your future. Tell her that nothing she says will change how you feel about her. Try to make her understand that it's curiosity about your past, not dissatisfaction with the present, that leads you to ask these questions. If it's still too painful for your mom, perhaps you have a grandparent who would be easier to talk to. Whatever you do, whatever you ask, be sure to do it lovingly. Sometimes adults want to avoid sad or hurtful memories. That's what your mom is doing.

It might be a good idea to talk to your pastor about this. Each and every situation is different. Only the individuals involved and people who know them well can decide what is best. Not knowing anything about your dad is just like having a piece of "unfinished business" nagging at you. You can't quite get it out of your mind. You shouldn't have to worry about this all by yourself. Once you and your mom can talk openly and honestly, you'll probably feel better. But be patient. This might take some time. Perhaps, if you can work through this together, you and your mother will be even closer.

## TEN

## "I Resent My Parents..."

● ● ● ● ● ● ● ● ●

*I began reading* New Girl in Town *just this morning, and I couldn't put it down. The story is so real, and I can very much relate to it. I'm a lot like Lexi. I often resent my parents for moving our family from the warmth and homeyness of a small town where I had many friends to the fast-paced action of city life.*

—Denise, age 16

Though you might not believe it, parents really don't make decisions just to drive their kids crazy! Usually that craziness is a byproduct of a decision actually made out of love and concern. You dislike your new home. Your parents forced you to move there. You miss your old friends, neighborhood, school, and house. As a result, you are angry with your parents.

Actually, I don't blame you. It's hard to make a big life-change. It was probably hard on your folks, too. It's just that parents have to make their decisions based on issues that teenagers don't often take into consideration.

Example: Parents have to ask these questions—"Will this move benefit our entire family?" "Will we have better jobs and be able to provide more easily for our children?" "Are we improving ourselves in life with this move?" "If I refuse this transfer, will I lose my job?" "Will this career move achieve one of the goals I (Mom/Dad) have set in life?" "Will our future be brighter there?"

Your parents wouldn't intentionally make a move that provided a poorer job and placed you in an inadequate school or a dangerous neighborhood. (Some of those things actually might happen, but parents wouldn't *plan* it that way!)

Try to keep in mind that people never try to make a *bad* move, only good ones. Your parents' intentions are good. That should make it a little easier to stop resenting their decision.

What's more, resentment hurts. It hurts *you* by souring you inside. It's like pouring vinegar into milk. Yuk! It curdles all the pleasant feelings you have and takes the fun out of the good things that might happen to you in this new move (new friends, a great school, a teacher you adore, a house with a bedroom just for you).

Resentment also hurts your relationship with your parents. You're so busy shooting them daggered looks and rolling your eyes every time they open their mouths to speak that you don't have fun with them anymore. Who needs to waste their time like that? Not you!

---

## Try to remember that people (parents included!) never intentionally make a bad decision.

---

Get rid of the bitterness you are feeling toward your parents for forcing you to move away from the home you loved. Talk to them. Tell them how you feel. Ask them to help you get over these feelings. Let them help you.

Give the new place a chance. Enjoy the things you couldn't enjoy in the country (museums, theme parks, concerts, malls, whatever appeals to you). Find *new* special things about this place. You might have to look hard at first, but I know you will find them. Best of all, you have friends everywhere—you just haven't met them all yet.

## ELEVEN

## "My Parents Are Too Strict..."

● ● ● ● ● ● ● ● ●

*My parents are really strict. I can't sit on the bed after it's made or go barefoot. I hate it. I love my parents, but I really think they're overly strict.*

—Rhonda, age 11

That *is* strict! But, without hearing your parents' side of the story, it's hard for me to say if I agree with their rules or not. The important thing is that you love your parents and want to please them. That's great. You're doing exactly what God desires of us.

You also have to give your folks credit for trying to do their best. My girls sometimes accuse me of *too much mothering.* They'd like it if I got so busy that I'd forget to pay attention to them for just a little while—but they'll have no such luck. I take my job as mother every bit as seriously as I do my job as wife and author. If you're lucky enough to have parents who care so much, you'll have to take a little of the bad with the good. That "bad" might include a few more rules and restrictions than you'd like.

It might help for you to understand *why* your parents have made the rules you must live by at your house. Rules and regulations don't make a whole lot of sense unless you understand *where* they are coming from. What's more, once you know *why* they feel the way they do, it will be easier for you to respect their wishes.

The only way you'll find out why your parents are so tough on these issues is to *ask* them.

Here's a warning, though: Don't inquire in an argumentative tone of voice. Simply and sincerely explain that you'd like to know why they think their rules are important. *Don't* come at them with the statement, "Nobody else lives like this!" That will put them on the defensive, and your conversation will come to an abrupt and unpleasant end. Also be aware of your body language. Your gestures and movements should be relaxed. You don't want to pick a fight—just get an answer.

Choose a time when everyone is in a good mood (after dessert is nice) and ask them to explain. (Try one question a day or week—don't overwhelm them!) You might be surprised. Maybe you'll agree with them once they state their position.

One unbreakable rule we have at our house is that whenever one of us leaves the house, we *must* leave a note for the others, saying where we've gone. That drives my youngest daughter crazy. "Nobody else has to leave a note!" she complains. "My friends can go anywhere they want and they don't have to be checking in like that."

Once I explained myself to her, however, she really couldn't argue with my reasoning. First of all, I don't believe that I'm the only parent in town who demands to know where her children are. Secondly, the rule I've made for my children also applies to *me*. I don't leave home without leaving word for the kids where I am and what time I'll be back. To me, it's common courtesy to do so, and I don't expect any less of myself than I do my children.

---

**See if you can see your parents' rules through *their* eyes. What are they trying to teach you with their rules?**

---

Your parents want to protect you from harm, teach you good things, and give you the very best in life. Once you understand where they are coming from, their strictness may be easier to accept. Sometimes you might even be able to negotiate a compromise. (Example: If one of my daughters forgets to leave a note, she doesn't have to run home to write one. If she can call my answering machine and leave a message, that's okay too. But when I can't find the girls or a message anywhere, *that's* when I get irritated! Fortunately, it doesn't happen often. We've learned a common courtesy at our house and we're all better for it.)

*What kind of music is Lexi listening to when she is with her friends or at the Hamburger Shack? Is it Christian or secular? What is wrong with secular music anyway?! My mom won't let me listen to it. I don't know why my parents don't want me to listen to that kind of music. I don't think my parents understand that I'm old enough not to do the things I hear!*

—Angela, age 13

I believe that where music is concerned, *words count.* Lots of beautiful music has been created to be enjoyed— both secular and Christian. It's probably not the music itself that upsets your mom, but the lyrics. Some lyrics are funny and sweet; others are offensive. I don't like sexually explicit or rough language, or unwholesome images portrayed in the music I listen to. When those songs come on, I'll probably switch stations. That's a choice that everyone can make.

Have you ever heard the saying, "You are what you eat?" It simply means that the type of food you put into your body determines the health of your body. It's known that too much fatty food causes an increase in certain types of cancers. Too much caffeine (as in coffee) can cause nervousness and sleeplessness. Broccoli and apples are healthy sources of vitamins and fiber. If you increase your intake of healthy foods and eat fewer unhealthy ones, it only makes sense that you'll be a healthier person.

## The saying "You are what you eat" applies to your thought life as well.

There's a parallel here with what you put into your mind. If you put junk into your mind, how can your mind help but be a junkyard? After all, the stuff you put in there has to go somewhere! Believe it or not, the Bible talks about this. (Amazing, isn't it, that all those years ago when music was played on flutes and timbrels that there would be a verse written that applies to rock music!) "Continue to think about the things that are good and worthy of praise. Think about the things that are true and honorable and right and pure and beautiful and respected" (Philippians 4:8).

In other words, put good, wholesome, healthy thoughts and images into your mind to make your mind wholesome and healthy!

Think of music with rough, offensive, or suggestive lyrics as greasy, artery-clogging, unhealthy fat. Don't put too much into your diet. It's not smart to fill your body or your mind with junk food! Remember, music itself isn't "bad" or "good." Just be wise about the messages you're hearing and filter out the unhealthy ones. That way you can make good choices with the radio dial.

If your mom isn't comfortable with allowing you to make these choices, then you should respect her wishes. She's trying to do her job—being the best mother she knows how to be. Besides, with the great Christian contemporary music that we have today, who needs the rock-and-roll stations!

*I have a problem with my parents. I have a sister and a brother. My mother makes me baby-sit for them even if I have something planned. Then she doesn't pay me as much as she pays another sitter to baby-sit for them. Plus, she won't let me go out in a group if there are guys in it. Could you help me on a way to approach them?*

—Courtney, age 11

If you can't *talk* to your mom, *write* to her! Tell her just what you told me. Tell her that you'd like to know in advance when she needs you to baby-sit so that you don't make other plans. Express your wish to be paid as much as another baby-sitter would be paid for the same work. Compose your letter thoughtfully and carefully, showing her how grown-up and responsible you are.

Here's a suggestion that might work for you. Tell (or write) your mom that if you can be paid full wages for three baby-sitting sessions, you'll do the fourth one for free. (Sort of like the "Buy Three, Get One Free" sales.)

"Why?" you ask. Because I feel that every person in a family should be responsible for helping out with some tasks in the family. Obviously baby-sitting is one of your responsibilities. Your mom knows this and that's probably why she pays you a little less. She expects you to help out with this particular task. She doesn't mean to cheat you out of fair wages. She's seeing your baby-sitting responsibilities as part of your family duties.

If she is willing to pay you what other sitters get for three out of four baby-sitting jobs, then not only will she be pleased to have you volunteer to care for your sister and brother without pay, you'll be less resentful about baby-sitting. After all, you'll get paid what you feel you are worth. You probably won't make any more money, but at least you'll feel better about the situation. (And you probably wouldn't mind sitting for free occasionally as long as you get paid the rest of the time.)

---

**Being in a family unit often means having to compromise, to negotiate, and most of all having to love without reservation.**

---

There are certain secrets to getting along in a family: (1) Don't hide bad feelings. Talk them out. See if they can be settled. (2) Be reasonable. Sometimes you get your way, sometimes you don't. If you can do these two things—if *everyone* in your family can do them—there will be fewer hurt feelings and more joy in being together.

## TWELVE

## "All My Friends Do It..."

● ● ● ● ● ● ● ● ●

*My parents think I'm too young for a boyfriend. (All my friends have one.) I'm twelve years old and in the sixth grade.*

—Darcy, age 12

I think I'll have to apologize in advance here because I'm going to sound like a mother . . . but that's part of what I am!

You're asking two questions here. One comes across loud and clear. The other is a little harder to pick out. I'll speak to the second issue first.

*All my friends have one. . . .* Here's the real issue. This is the oldest bargaining chip known to teenagers. This is just another version of *"Everyone else gets to!"*

My daughters try this out on me every once in a while (just to see if I'm paying attention, or to see if somehow, miraculously, I've changed my mind about a long-standing opinion). The latest version at my house is *"Everybody* dates at twelve!"

What would I discover if I responded by saying, *"Ev-*

*erybody?* Really? Imagine that! I think I'll call a few mothers and find out. . . ."

I'd probably see some back-peddling on that statement and hear a plea that went something like this—"No! Don't *call* anyone. Motherrr."

You see, what seems like "everybody" to you is really only a small percentage of twelve-year-olds. I'm not unrealistic. I know that kids pair up whenever they can, but I can't say I approve of it.

Now, before you shut down and quit reading because I sound like your mom and dad, let me try to explain *why* parents have such a violent response to the idea of twelve-year-old girls having boyfriends.

One of the big words parents will use in trying to explain their position on this issue is *maturity.*

Don't get me wrong. Twelve-year-olds can be very mature, but often that maturity comes in stages.

At twelve, a girl can be very mature *physically.* She can be as tall as she's ever going to grow. The physical maturity can be like that of a sixteen-year-old. Emotional maturity can follow several years after physical maturation is complete. It's emotional immaturity that alarms parents. They don't want their daughters dating—and making the decisions involved therein—until they are sure that they are emotionally ready.

Unfortunately, emotional maturity doesn't come on a time schedule. Some twelve-year-olds can be quite emotionally mature, while I've known thirty-year-olds who haven't got it yet!

I'd like to explain boyfriends (dating, sex, that whole issue) by using a time line.

At one end of the time line you see a girl's first interest in boys. That usually happens at twelve or younger. At the other end of the line is sexual intimacy/intercourse, which should come after marriage. That, ultimately, is what this first budding interest in boys will lead to. (But I just want a boyfriend, you're saying, not all that other . . ."stuff!")

Once a girl begins to notice the opposite sex (i.e., boys), her parents begin to imagine her careening rapidly to the

# TIME LINE:

— *First interest in the opposite sex*

— *"Hmmm, I guess all boys aren't creeps after all."*

— *"Wow! Jake is pretty cute."*

— *"I'm not pretty. I'm not popular. I'm going to be an old maid."*

— *"I think he likes me. I know I like him."*

— *Group activities, with both sexes hanging out together.*

— *Double dates*

— *Dates alone*

— *"I think I'm in love."*

— *Steady dating*

— *"I know I'm in love."*

— *Marriage*

— *Sexual intimacy/intercourse*

other end of the time line and getting involved in sexual activity, an intimacy that should be reserved for marriage. (Granted, you could tell them that this won't happen overnight, but it's hard for parents to see their precious little daughters growing up. What's more, they've been through this already when they were teens, and they know how quickly things can happen and how easily bad or destructive decisions can be made.)

While your parents are panicking, you are seeing yourself stuck at the *beginning* of the time line for the rest of your life. You are afraid that you aren't pretty, that you won't be popular, that a boy (any boy) will never notice you.

Frankly, both views are wrong. An early interest in boys doesn't mean you'll be married by high-school graduation. That's not any more likely to happen than your never sparking the interest of someone of the male gender. Still, there's more danger from being in the dating world too early than there is in being unnoticed by boys for a few years.

Starting to have boyfriends at too young an age gives you more opportunity to make mistakes and poor choices about relationships. Once you start with that time line (an interest in the opposite sex), you will move slowly (or maybe quickly) toward the other end of the line (sexual intimacy/intercourse, which should be reserved for marriage).

I realize how *bizarre* that might sound to someone who is twelve, but your parents know it's true. They've traveled that time line too—from first love to the deep, intimate relationship that produced you. That's why adults always recommend starting the process at an age when you can handle whatever situation you might get into.

And what kind of situation might that be? Use your imagination. You are invited to a boy-girl party. Once you get there, you discover that there are no parents at home. Everyone is pairing up, until you feel like you've stepped onto Noah's Ark. There's even a boy for you. The lights are turned down. People begin to drift into the back rooms of the house and you realize this boy expects to do the same thing that the couple lying horizontally on the couch is doing. What do you do?

It might be easy to think to yourself, "I'll call my parents." It might be harder to actually *do* it. After all, everyone will know that you are the one who ruined *everyone's* fun. You'll be the one who gets the party hostess in trouble with her mom and dad. Even if you don't tell your parents everything, the kids will think of you as a party pooper, a tattletale, or a coward. Can you handle that?

Suddenly, you are faced with a rather difficult decision. There's this little problem of wanting to be popular . . . and the boy is pretty cute . . . and if you don't listen to your conscience (which is probably screaming at the top of its lungs at you) . . .

This scenario sounds like a lot of trouble to me. Who needs it? All sorts of questions about right and wrong come up about sex once you get involved in boy-girl relationships. Usually these debates occur in the backseat of a car or in someone's family room when the lights are out. Don't get involved too early. You have your entire life before you. It's unlikely that you'll go through life without ever being kissed by the opposite sex.

---

## Dating at too young an age only provides more opportunity for mistakes. Who needs it?

---

My mother always told me, "There are plenty of fish in the sea." She didn't really want me to go fishing, but she did want me to realize that there's a whole "sea" full of guys out there. I didn't have to panic if I didn't catch one right away. Maybe an even bigger and better one would swim by later!

When you *do* start dating, use Todd and Lexi from Cedar River Daydreams as an example of what a teen relationship should be. Todd and Lexi are *first and foremost* the best of friends. They have purposely left out the sexual intimacy and consequent tension that destroys most high-school relationships. An occasional kiss may be okay, but be careful not to allow it to move past there, or you will jeopardize the most important part—*friendship*.

Your parents want to protect you. They want your interests and activities to stay age-appropriate (that means they don't want you to rush things—like romance). Believe it or not, you are lucky to have parents who are willing to say no. They say no because they care.

I can almost hear you saying, "Yeah, right! I'm supposed to feel lucky that my parents don't want me to have a life?"

In this case, yes. If you were sixteen, my answer to you would be entirely different. At twelve, you don't need a boyfriend to complicate your life. My suggestion to you comes from Proverbs 13:1, "A wise son (or daughter) takes his father's advice. . . ."

## THIRTEEN

# "My Dad's Going Through a Mid-Life Crisis..."

● ● ● ● ● ● ● ● ●

*My mother says my father is going through mid-life crisis. I don't understand. Why does he act the way he does?*

—Jodi, age 11

A "mid-life crisis" is a difficult concept for a teenager to understand. (Frankly, it's difficult for *anyone* to understand until they've been through it.) When you are a teenager, your whole life is ahead of you. You've lived only thirteen or fourteen of the seventy to eighty years you hope to live. That's less than twenty percent of your entire life! The possibilities of things you can do and see and be seem limitless. You look forward to high-school graduation, college, falling in love for the very first time, starting a family, traveling . . . the list is endless. You just *know* that you'll be able to accomplish what you set out to do. Your goals are high. Your confidence about achieving them is higher still.

That's a great position in which to be. Young people are lulled into complacency, thinking that they have all the time in the world to get done what they wish to achieve.

71

Years pass. Then, suddenly, (it shouldn't be a surprise, but it usually is) a person realizes that he or she is no longer in his teens, or twenties, or even thirties. He's forty-five years old! That's the age he used to think of as *ancient*. He remembers his father at forty-five. His grandfather was forty-five when he was born. His kids are growing up. He no longer sees 80% of his life stretch on before him. He's used up over half of his eighty years. He's halfway through his life. Eeek! It's time for a *mid-life crisis.*

---

### What's the key to avoiding a confusing mid-life crisis? *Live your life right the first time!*

---

Your dad is in this position. He's reached an age at which he's started to become reflective. When a man looks back over his life and sees what choices he's made, what things he's done, sometimes he feels it's not enough. Perhaps he didn't finish college as he'd planned. Or maybe he didn't become president of his company. Many men see that they haven't accomplished all they'd hoped and dreamed, and wrongly begin to see themselves as failures.

In a desperate attempt to recapture some of what they feel they've missed, men will sometimes try to recapture their youth. They'll try to "relive" those experiences they think they missed the first time through. That's when some men will buy a flashy little sports car to make them feel young again. Sometimes they will decide that dating a younger woman will help prove (to both themselves and others) that they still "have it" (that youthful attraction to the opposite sex that teenagers take so much for granted). Trying to recapture lost youth makes people do strange, illogical things.

Until he gets through this phase, (see, even adults go through phases!) and begins to realize what wonderful, rewarding, worthwhile qualities come with middle-age, your dad will be hard to understand. Because one can't really relive a life, he's bound to be frustrated. Until he appreciates his own worth at the age he is right now, he will be unpredictable and difficult to live with.

When will this be over?

That's different for every person and every situation.

What can you do? Two things. First, you can pray for him, for your family, and for yourself. God can give you some amazing support if you only tap into it by asking for His help. Secondly, you must *take care of yourself.* If you are frightened, confused, and lonely, *get some help.* Go to your mom, pastor, school counselor, or some adult you can talk to. Ask them to listen to you. Tell them about your feelings and ask them the questions you need answered. You can't control or change your parents. You can only be responsible for yourself.

Does all this sound rather dreadful? I suppose it does, but, as with most difficult things, there is a lesson to be learned. *Live your own life right the first time!*

That might sound silly to a teenager, but I'm a big believer in having as few regrets as possible about things you've said or done. Make good choices. Set worthy goals. Don't do anything you'll wish you could "undo" later. Think before you speak—especially if you plan to say something hurtful. Enjoy every day. Look for the good in it and not the bad. Get to know Christ early in your life because He's the best Companion you can have as you grow and mature. He's the one Friend who's sure to stick with you through it all.

Everyone has things in their lives they wish they hadn't done or said. But, if you learn early to keep your little corner of the universe in order, decorated with kindness, thoughtfulness, trustworthiness, and honesty, perhaps you'll avoid some of the unhappiness and regret from which your father is suffering.

*Lately, my dad's been stressed out. He keeps it to himself and it causes problems. He's been so stressed, he grinds his teeth in his sleep.*

—Melody, age 13

There's a lot of that going around—stress, I mean.

We're living in a tough, competitive, high-pressure world. Your dad has to work in that setting every day. He has to provide for his family, satisfy his boss, and worry about the state of the economy, just to name a few stresses.

When Mom or Dad is tense, everyone in the household feels it. Even though your parents try not to, they'll often take some of the stress out on you. You can't change the outside forces that are causing your parents' stress. All you can do is make an effort not to cause them any more stress at home.

These suggestions won't make a major change in your family situation, but they can't hurt:

1. Bake Dad's favorite cookies and give them to him on a plate with a note that says, "I love you, Dad."

2. Clean your room without being told.

3. Wash the car, mow the grass, carry out garbage, feed the dog, or do some other chore that usually falls on Dad's shoulders.

4. Smile at him in the hallway when you pass.

5. Give him hugs and tell him you're doing it "just because I love you."

6. Turn your worry over to God, because even though you can't ease your father's stress, He can. "If he stumbles, he will not fall, because the Lord holds his hand" (Psalm 37:24).

## FOURTEEN

## "My Father Lost His Job ..."

● ● ● ● ● ● ● ● ●

*My father lost his job and my family is having a hard time.*
—Rita, age 16

*We don't have any money.*
—Tia, age 11

*My mom had to go to work.*
—Dana, age 12

*My dad is depressed.*
—Polly, age 16

*I've been in a Christian school my whole life. Next year I have to go to a public school because my dad is getting laid off from work.*
—Randi, age 13

These situations are familiar to many. In a troubled

**75**

national economy, many people are losing their jobs. In such cases all family members suffer, not just the unemployed parents. What's more, it pushes everyone into feelings of helplessness and despair.

Though you have no control over your parents' financial status, your needs are still important. If there is something that is very important to you (being on a sports team, or in a club, or having music lessons), and it doesn't appear your family can afford it, talk to your parents about it anyway. Sometimes, with some combined creative thinking, you and your parents may be able to come up with a way to provide those things.

Perhaps it will mean your finding a part-time job, or doing more baby-sitting, but that's a small price to pay for something you want a great deal. Maybe there are scholarships available, or work-study programs. Who knows, unless you try?

Remember, however, that *you are not responsible* for your parents' financial situation. Leave that problem to the adults. If it worries you, talk to your parents about it, but don't blame yourself.

---

### You are not the reason for this situation. You are not the one who must find a way out.

---

"But what can *I* do?" you ask.

Frankly, not much. Your dad/mom will have to find another job. Your family will have to cut corners financially until he/she does. That's the reality. There are really only two or three things you can do:

1. Understand the situation.
2. Stay cheerful, stay helpful, stay up-beat.
3. Trust the adults. They are there to take care of you. They are doing the best they can.

Did you know that some experts now believe that moods and attitudes can be "caught" just like a cold or the

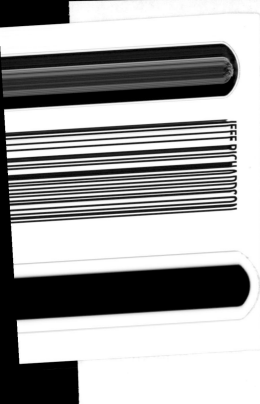

oomy if someone in a group is per-
optimistic. Maybe, for now, you're
he carrier of this "cheerful virus."
catches it. Breathe smiles and good
ace.

## FIFTEEN

## "Kids Tease Me Because We're Rich...." "Kids Tease Me Because We're Poor...."

● ● ● ● ● ● ● ● ●

What do these conflicting statements tell you? *That kids like to tease!* It doesn't matter if you are rich or poor. At some time in your growing-up years, you'll get teased about something. Kids are great judges of character and personality. They can, without forethought, find your weakest point, figure out what will bug you the very most, and tease you about it.

Actually, getting teased isn't even the issue. *How you handle that teasing is.*

Maybe you have a nose like Pinocchio's, or ears like Dumbo. That makes you a perfect target for teasing. When some little monster comes up to remind you to put a hat on so the wind doesn't get in your ears and cause you to fly away, you have two choices:

One, you can get angry (or hurt, or teary-eyed). That's *exactly* what your tormentor wants you to do. Presto, you've for any situation.

People who tease someone who is poor, for instance, do it to make themselves feel big. It's a sure sign that they are insecure themselves. Those who tease someone who is rich believe they are doing it to humble the rich person and bring him down to size. (And they are probably jealous.)

Minda, Lexi's number-one headache, is famous for her hurtful comments and constant teasing. But if you read between the lines, you'll know that Minda is really very insecure. Her homelife is pretty rotten, and she cuts other people down in order to draw attention to herself and make herself feel important *because she doesn't feel that way at home.*

---

### People who tease others do it out of insecurity. Don't fall into the trap they set.

---

Next time a tormentor approaches you, try saying something like, "I really like your new outfit." That way, you've made the insecure person feel good about himself/herself, without your having to be the doormat.

If you refuse to fall into the trap they set, you'll avoid a lot of hassles. The Bible says it best: "A gentle answer will calm a person's anger. But an unkind answer will cause more anger" (Proverbs 15:1).

Even if you are itching to "tell that creep off," don't.

*Dear Judy,*

The words won't taste nearly as good in your mouth as you might think. What's more, as Christians, we need to allow our faith to permeate every part of our lives—even our conflicts.

## SIXTEEN

## "My Mom Is Sick..."
●●●●●●●●●

*My mom has multiple sclerosis. I'm kept busy helping my mom, even though she doesn't have it bad. She can walk, although not well sometimes. She has some energy returning. We're praying that she'll have a remission and that it won't get worse when the re-mission is over.*

—Cory, age 14

*When I was twelve, my mother was put in the hospital because of a car accident. The doctors said she would not live twenty-four hours, but she was a fighter and pulled through. God was my friend through all this. I never really had a friend until I started to talk to God.*

—Maria, age 13

*My mother was in a serious car accident. Sometimes I wonder why God didn't stop the other driver from making a big mistake. Judy, I've tried talking to Him about this, but I can't. She broke many bones in her body. I wouldn't have made it through those hours at the hospital if it hadn't been for our pastor and his wife. The hours seemed to be stretched for miles. (I hope you aren't getting bored. I just need to talk to someone.)*

*Judy, thanks for being a great listener. I needed that. You're like a shoulder to cry on, only in letters though. Sorry to have taken up so much of your time. I'm glad you took the time to listen, even if you're really busy. You're the only one that really ever listens to me.*

—Brenda, age 12

No time in a child or teenager's life is more frightening than when a parent is seriously ill. It may be the very first time that person has considered death or really realized that *it happens to everyone. Even my parents. Even me.*

Like so many other things in life, illness is also out of our control. We can eat healthy foods, and buckle our seat belts, of course, but we can't affect the drunk driver careening down the highway toward us, or change the genetic code that passes on certain illnesses within a family. Once a teenager is thrown into this world of stark reality, he/she has to have ways to cope.

One of these ways is denial: "Mom's fine. No big deal. Don't worry about it."

Another is to act like Chicken Little when she thought the sky was falling, and panic: "She's going to die! I just know it! How can she do this to me?"

A third way to cope is to respond with anger and rebellion: "I'm going to reject her before she dies and rejects me. So there."

Most of us fall somewhere in the middle of these extremes, and keep most of our fears and concerns to ourselves and struggle to put on a happy face. After all, this is a worry that is so *BIG AND IMPORTANT* that we can't talk about it easily to anyone. This isn't any better a response than the others.

---

**When important issues are troubling you, find someone to talk to.**

---

It might seem like an impossible task to walk up to an adult and say, "Will you help me? I need to talk to someone," but it's no harder than suffering alone. Even though it might help to talk to a friend or peer, it's important to talk to someone who can give you some facts.

Facts? Why?

Because knowing the honest truth about a situation is a whole lot less scary than what you can conjure in your mind. If you think about an illness long enough, you can imagine a lot of blood, gore, pain, and trouble. After all, you're creative. Your mind can take you to places you really don't want to go. It's better to find out about the illness and know how it will act and affect your family than to imagine something even worse. Besides, honesty and straightforwardness in a family are the best ways to deal with trouble.

If there's trouble in a family, the kids in that family will know it whether anyone discusses the problems with them or not. You can sense when people are worried about something, even though they may be denying that anything is wrong.

If having multiple sclerosis means a roller-coaster ride of good and bad days, you can be prepared for that. If surgery means a great deal of discomfort for your parent, you'll be a lot less alarmed when she's more short-tempered than usual. Knowing the facts also gives you the opportunity to learn how to help. The best prescription a child can offer her parent is affection, patience, and a willingness to be a gopher. (You know, "Please 'go-fer' my glasses, and bring back a dish of pudding while you're at it; 'go-fer' the mail, and find this morning's paper. . . .")

The Bible talks about sickness and healing. Jesus healed many people while He was still on earth. My favorite passage about healing doesn't really talk about *physical* healing, however. "Christ carried our sins in his body on the cross. He did this so that we would stop living for sin and start living for what is right. And we *are healed* because of his wounds" (1 Peter 2:24). This sort of healing is made possible through our relationship with Christ.

As always, Christians have an advantage over non-believers where health issues are concerned. They have Someone to talk to when it's dark and quiet and the scary thoughts overtake them.

Jesus is history's greatest healer. He can heal what's wrong with you spiritually, mentally, *and* physically, if necessary. Bring Him into your struggles. He cares about you and for your family. There's no problem too big or too small for God. He knows how to handle them all.

## SEVENTEEN

## "Someone in My Family Isn't a Christian..."

● ● ● ● ● ● ● ●

*Everybody in my immediate family is a Christian except my dad.*

—Marla, age 12

*I come from a broken home. I live with my mom. My mom's a strong Christian, but my dad doesn't even believe God is alive.*

—Johanna, age 14

*My parents are divorced, and I live with my dad and stepmom. They're very devoted Christians, and so is my brother. My real mom, on the other hand, has no religion, and isn't even looking for one.*

—Brianna, age 13

First and foremost, don't give up hope. Acts 16:31 says, "Believe in the Lord Jesus and you will be saved—you and all the people in your house." That means that the faith of *one person* in a household or family can influence all the people who live with him/her. Of course, you aren't doing it alone. The faith you have comes from God. He takes care of you so well that even your faith to believe in Him is God's gift to you! Pray that the others at your house will receive that gift as well.

We don't always know what it is that finally makes a person change his heart and mind about God. That's okay. The issue is between that individual and God. All you can do is try to smooth the process along—grease the wheels with prayer, so to speak. Live as you are supposed to live and it will speak volumes. You are part of a team and God is on your side. That sounds like a winning combination to me!

*I just finished reading your Cedar River Daydreams Book #6,* Broken Promises. *In the book, I noticed that you talk a lot about God. My family does not go to church at all, and I want to. I really want to be saved and to be baptized. It is very important to me. But my parents don't seem to care. I've talked to them about going to church before, but they just seem to forget about it. I'm only twelve and I can't exactly go by myself. What should I do about it? I've gone to church a couple of times with friends, but I don't really know anyone who goes steadily. Please help me!*

—Cathy, age 12

You are in an awkward, but not impossible spot. First, try telling your parents how you feel. Ask them to take you to church. Remind them on Saturday night so that they will have time to plan. If that doesn't work out, perhaps you can go again with your friends. Keep your eyes and ears open. Find out what kind of youth group your church has. Join that. Make friends there. If and when you feel comfortable, talk to the pastor about your wishes.

Is there an adult you know who would be willing to let you ride to church with his or her family? Do your neighbors attend church? Grandparents? Perhaps you can approach the parents of your friends and ask for a ride.

If all this seems just too difficult, don't give up. After

all, you have access to the "instruction book" for that church already. It's the Bible. What's more, there are many devotional books available for teens so that you can study and have your questions answered right at home in your own room. Though the church is God's house, He's not limited by walls or structures. "The Lord is with you when you are with him . . ." (2 Chronicles 15:2). Isn't that a great thought? The Creator of the Universe makes *house calls*! If you ask Him, He will come to you—any time, day or night.

---

### You don't have to go to God to be near Him. He also comes to you.

---

In fact, He *wants* you to "seek" (that means to look for or call upon) Him. "The Lord is good to those who put their hope in him. He is good to those who look to him for help" (Lamentations 3:25). He just wants you to look for Him sincerely—"When you search for me with all your heart, you will find me! I will let you find me . . ." (Jeremiah 29:13–14). Neat, huh?

Don't worry anymore. Just get started where you can. God can work on your heart and your mind wherever you are. Just be open and receptive and He won't disappoint you.

Perhaps I should explain the message that you'll get at church and from those devotionals. You'll hear a lot about being saved by Christ. It's the "Good News" of the gospel that Christians like to talk about.

About two thousand years ago, Jesus Christ, who is God's Son, came to the earth to die for the sins of each one of us. Christ died in our place. His death gave us the opportunity to be forgiven for all we've done wrong. Once you recognize that you are a sinner—"All people have sinned and are not good enough for God's glory" (Romans 3:23), you will no doubt want to repent of your sins.

What does repenting mean? It means admitting you've done something wrong and making the decision not to do it again. You might say, "I'm sorry, God. I'll try my hardest not to do that anymore!"

When you ask Christ to become a part of your life, you aren't going to want to do some of those things you've done in the past anyway. They aren't going to feel right or appropriate anymore. Once you recognize that Someone was willing to die for you so that you wouldn't have to take your own punishment for the things you've done wrong, you're going to be so happy and grateful that giving up your old habits won't be so hard.

That's the Good News of the Cross. God, our perfect Creator, wants you to be with Him in heaven someday. He sent His Son Jesus (whom He loves very much) to take your punishment by dying on the cross. Because Jesus died for you (and for me and for everyone), if we accept this great gift, we too will go to heaven.

The salvation story is really amazing, but do you know what I think is even more incredible? *If you had been the only person on the face of the earth, Jesus would still have died for you!* Think about it. He was willing to die for all of us, but He was also willing to die for just *one* of us! That's how much He cares for each and every person. You didn't know how much you were loved, did you? Enjoy it. Cherish it. It's the greatest gift a human being can ever receive.

*It's hard not getting caught up with the things of the world. Believe me, I know. My mom left our church. Now I'm free to do anything with people at school.*

*I've got a lot of decisions I have to make because my home environment isn't very encouraging. I'm the only one who goes to church in my family, and my house is filled with cursing. I don't like being around it!*

*I've had offers to go and live with relatives, and that's what I want, but my dad would never let me. All I can say is I am praying for the right thing to do.*

—Jessica, age 13

There's a passage in the Bible for just such a problem. I always find it amazing that a book written so many years ago has something to say to us today. Ephesians was written in the year *60.* That's 60 years after the birth of Christ and over 1,930 years ago! Of course, I really *shouldn't* be surprised. God is as in touch with His children now as He was a thousand years ago.

Here's the passage:

> Be strong in the Lord and in his great power. Wear the full armor of God. Wear God's armor so that you can fight against the devil's evil tricks. . . . We are fighting against the spiritual powers of evil in the heavenly world. That is why you need to get God's full armor. Then on the day of evil you will be able to stand strong. And when you have finished the whole fight, you will still be standing. So stand strong, with the belt of truth tied around your waist. And on your chest wear the protection of right living. And on your feet wear the Good News of peace to help you stand strong. And also use the shield of faith. With that you can stop all the burning arrows of the Evil One. Accept God's salvation to be your helmet. And take the sword of the spirit—that sword is the teaching of God. (Ephesians 6:10–17)

Now what, exactly, does that mean? It means that there is a spiritual battle going on inside you. (That's why it's so hard, as you put it, to not "get caught up in the things of the world.") Everyone is taking sides in this battle. You've chosen to be on God's side. That's why Satan feels free to take pot-shots at you. He delights in tempting you to see what you will do.

You don't *really* have to put on armor to fight this battle—at least not the kind you see in museums. The pieces of armor you have to use are *truth, God's love, the Good News of Christ's sacrifice for us—salvation—and God's Word.*

Think of it like this—get dressed in God's armor every morning, and Satan's arrows and bullets and stones (the unkind words, the feelings of doubt and depression, the temptations we know we shouldn't let get the best of us) will be bouncing off you all day long! God doesn't promise that it will always be easy, but He does promise to be with you every step of the way.

## EIGHTEEN

## "My Father Abused My Mother and Me…"

● ● ● ● ● ● ● ● ●

I started to write this section with a nervous knot in my stomach, because this is so difficult an issue that I hardly know where to begin. I don't claim to be a professional at this, only a writer, a mother, and someone with a respectable amount of common sense. Therefore, without wanting to seem as though I'm "passing the buck" on this, my first, best, and only advice about abuse situations is to *get professional help.* I can't judge from my office and my typewriter how much trouble a child or family is in. *I just know that it is never right to abuse.*

Parents are put on this earth to love, nurture, and cherish their children. In Ephesians 6:4 it says, "Fathers, do not make your children angry, but raise them with the training and teaching of the Lord." Anger and frustration should never be a part of discipline. Discipline should spring from a loving, nurturing concern for a child's well-being. Parents should treat their children as our heavenly Father would treat us. How can a child know or trust a heavenly Father if his/her earthly father is cruel or abusive?

*Get help. This is too big a problem for you to manage on your own.* As you read on, you'll see what I mean.

*My name is Kelsey. I read the Cedar River Daydreams series. I am eleven years old, and I love them. In each story there are a lot of things to think about. I just finished reading #7,* Silent Tears No More, *in which Nicole, the girl Binky baby-sits for, gets abused. I'm glad I read it because it helped me to understand how my dad might work. You see, all my life I've been verbally and physically abused. My dad is a very sick man. He must always get his way.*

*He swore all the time and would make Mom and me work while he sat in front of the TV.*

*My dad would say to me, "Don't go tell this to anyone. What happens at home, stays at home." So I kept my mouth shut. I went to school with bruises he'd given me. I would lie or make up excuses for why I had the bruises. The abusing started when I was a tiny baby. Whenever my mom tried to stop him, he would hit her and tell her to shut up.*

*He brainwashed my mom and me by telling us we were stupid and that he was always right. I had to apologize to him whenever I got hurt in an accident. He says there's no such thing as accidents. He would swear every night and hit my mom and me. Finally we couldn't take it anymore.*

*We left him.*

*Now I am going to counseling and have visitation with my dad once a week for an hour and a half. Mom and Dad are going to settlement court to see who gets permanent custody of me and what visitation rights my dad has. Then they will get divorced. I hope I never have to see my dad again. I'm scared he will get custody or regular visitation. Real scared.*

*P.S. Could you please write back and tell me some ways maybe not to be so worried?*

—Kelsey, age 12

Parents do not have the right to hurt their children. It is not God's wish, and it is illegal in our country. Unfortunately, children do not always know this—especially when they have been raised in an abusive environment.

A father or mother who abuses his or her child is mentally ill. Disturbed parents might think they are "disciplining" a child when they are actually abusing him/her.

If you are in this situation, *you must protect yourself.* Get out. *TELL SOMEONE WHAT IS HAPPENING TO YOU!* This won't be easy. It might be very painful to admit that someone you love and who is supposed to love you is hurting you. Still, the hurting must stop.

Who should you tell? That depends on your situation. I realize how scary this is, so if you can find someone you're comfortable with, that will help. Is there a *teacher* who is especially nice? Does your school have a *school counselor*? Is there a *minister* or *priest* you could talk to? *Doctors* will also listen to your problem. Every situation is different, but perhaps your *non-abusive parent* or a *trusted relative* will take action.

I understand that this will be hard—very hard. But you must protect yourself from harm.

How can you not worry so much? It's difficult. Worry creeps up on you in the night when you want to sleep and makes you imagine terrible things that might never happen. There are two people you can talk to who should be able to help you with your concerns. First, talk to your counselor or social worker. Tell them how frightened you are. Ask them to speak on your behalf to the judge. They are not afraid to say the things you might not be willing to voice. Second, talk to God. He's the One who can help you manage the worry that sneaks up on you in the night. He's the one who can get right into your head and whisper, "I am the Lord your God. I am holding your right hand. And I tell you, 'Don't be afraid, I will help you' " (Isaiah 41:13).

---

**If you are being abused, your number one priority must be to protect yourself. *Tell someone you trust what is happening to you.***

---

*My parents always call me a liar and hit me for no reason. They try their best to get on my nerves. I've tried praying, but nothing has happened. I'm still praying, but I need someone else to help me to pray. Please pray for me.*

—Paige, age 10

Your family sounds like a family in trouble. Your parents may have things going on in their lives that make them short-tempered, irritable, and suspicious. Unless those issues are resolved, things probably won't get any better. I'd recommend that you and your family get some counseling.

I almost hate to say that to a teenager, because I realize that the idea of forcing a family into counseling seems like an insurmountable task. Still, if someone doesn't cry out for help, the problem won't go away. It may only grow worse.

I'd depend on a pastor or school counselor in a case like this, because they can call your parents and tell them that they'd like to talk to you as a family. They are professionals and can take the burden of this problem from your shoulders. It's too big a load for you to carry alone.

## NINETEEN

## "My Friend Says Her Parents Beat Her..."

● ● ● ● ● ● ● ● ●

*I have a friend who isn't a Christian. Her mother works all day. One day my friend came home from school and her father was drunk (he gets drunk often). Her mother was not at home. He got really mad at her for nothing and started beating her up. He tore her jacket and pulled out a lot of her hair. She came over to my house and asked me what to do. I told her she could stay over at my house for the night. She is thirteen years old, but she looks about fifteen. Her father always compliments everyone else and puts her down. What should I do? Could you work out this problem in the Cedar River Daydreams? That way she could read about her own problem.*

—Amy, age 13

This would, indeed, be the type of problem one of the kids at Cedar River might face, but books take a long time to write, and your friend needs to tell her mother about her problem *now.*

Consider this an emergency. Encourage your friend to talk to her mom. She should refuse to stay alone with her father until he quits drinking and joins a group, such as Alcoholics Anonymous.

Alateen is a group for the children of alcoholics. Look in the phone book under Alcoholics Anonymous. They can provide support and information for your friend.

You have been a good friend to this girl. It's important that she know that she has a place to stay if she is caught in such a situation again. Unfortunately, however, a safe haven isn't enough. Her mom must begin to fix what has gone wrong in the family.

*I have a friend called Mallory. She told me and a few other friends that her mother locks her in a closet and hits her. I am quite worried about this. I told her to tell someone about it, like a teacher, but she said no! as if she were scared. Please write back to me and give me some advice about what to do. Mallory isn't a Christian, and I don't think she would understand. She is a bit slow and always gets teased by people.*

—Nancy, age 11

*Before the beginning of summer, my friend, Leah, told me her mom beat her until she bled. She told me not to tell anyone. I've met her mom before. She seems normal, but you can never tell by the way a person looks. PLEASE GIVE ME ADVICE.*

—Cynthia, age 10

Kids are always afraid to "tell" on their parents, but there are certain secrets that are dangerous to keep. If your friend's parent does something so troubling as to lock her daughter in a closet or beat her until she bleeds, *that parent is out of control and needs help.* No parent—when they are thinking clearly and sanely—would ever want to hurt their child so badly it might kill them, but, frankly, it can happen. At *best,* your friend will carry the memories of the cruelty with her every day for the rest of her life. At worst, she could be scarred, mutilated, or killed.

---

**If you have a friend who is being abused, talk to your own mom and dad. Ask them to help you. This is too big a problem to carry around by yourself.**

---

If a friend makes you promise not to tell something and then drops a bombshell like this in your lap, you've got a big problem. It's my opinion that if a secret is *so awful* that no one is ever to know about it, it's the type of secret that requires help for the people involved.

If someone wants you to keep a secret, tell them, "I'm not promising anything until I hear the secret first. If it's something really bad I might have to tell my parents."

Now the ball is back in your friend's court. *She'll* have to decide if she wants to share that secret, knowing how you feel.

I wish I had an easy answer for your problem, but there isn't one. Families often hide their secrets well. That's why your statement, "She seems normal, but you can never tell by the way a person looks," is so sad and so true. "Nice" looking people rob banks and steal cars. "Normal" looking people have killed other human beings. Mass murderers have been described by unknowing neighbors as "nice, quiet, normal" guys. You can't judge a person by how he or she looks. And just because they are someone's mother or father doesn't mean they know how to treat their children correctly.

The answer is both simple and difficult. If you or someone you know is in this kind of trouble, I'll list the sources of help again: the non-abusive parent (sometimes they hate what's going on so much that they choose to ignore what's happening. If so, you'll have to find someone else to help you), pastor or priest, teacher, school counselor, trusted adult friend or relative, doctor, or government agencies such as child welfare and social services.

Not every adult can give you the help you need. If the

first person you turn to gives you advice that doesn't feel right, go to someone else. That's the only way your family can get back on track. There's no shame in asking for help. It's the right thing to do.

## TWENTY

# "I've Been Sexually Abused by a Family Member..."

● ● ● ● ● ● ● ● ●

*I can relate to* Silent Tears No More *because I have been sexually abused by my uncle. After I told my parents, we have found that others have been badly abused also. It seems hard to believe this has happened to my family. Your book helped me to realize that we aren't the only ones in this situation. I would appreciate it if you would pray for me.*

—Dana, age 13

You are certainly not alone! Sadly, *many* others have found themselves in similar situations. You are to be congratulated for going to your parents. Some girls and boys would be so ashamed of what had happened to them that they would try to keep the secret to themselves. They don't realize that they have *nothing to be ashamed of*! You are all *innocent victims.*

You've had a terrible thing happen to you, but it sounds as though you are beginning to heal. As time passes, your memories and thoughts about this incident will fade slightly and become fewer and further between.

Someday your smiles and laughter will return and the dark thoughts about what has happened will recede into the background of your memory.

Many people have had similar things happen to them and have come through it and gone on to lead happy, healthy, productive lives. Don't let that experience hold you back. If you ever have nightmares or flashbacks or recurring thoughts about what happened to you, don't be afraid to talk to your parents or counselor about it. The people who are trained to help and counsel you will not discuss what has happened to you or give out your name. You don't have to worry about your friends "finding out" things about your private life.

---

**We need to keep *mentally* as well as *physically* healthy in order to be the best possible people we can be.**

---

I'm convinced that God has wonderful, special plans for each and every one of us. With His help, you can be ready to do whatever He wishes.

## TWENTY – ONE

## "My Grandfather Lives With Us..."

● ● ● ● ● ● ● ● ●

*My grandpa lives with me and my family. Sometimes I have a lot of trouble trying to be nice to him. I get really frustrated sometimes because he lives with us.*

—Rachel, age 11

Don't feel badly because you get frustrated with your grandfather. Think of it this way—he's probably frustrated with you too! Just as you might think he's cranky and bossy, he may believe that you are noisy and have too much freedom for a girl your age. After all, there is probably a fifty- or sixty-year age difference between the two of you. It would be a surprise if you thought alike all the time. Still, God wants us to respect our elders.

---

**In America we aren't used to having several generations living in the same house. That means you have a special set of circumstances at your home that might take some extra effort on your part.**

---

It's not easy to share your home and parents with another person. In fact, it could just about drive you *nuts* if you let it—especially if you and that other person don't get along.

So what are you going to do about it? You could grit your teeth, stuff your irritation and anger down inside yourself and stay frustrated, or, you could try to improve your situation.

Exactly what is it that frustrates you? Is it having to share your parents with him? Is it having a third parent who bosses you around and lectures you when you don't do what he thinks is right? Or perhaps he's not well and complains a lot, and that gets on your nerves.

Think about whatever it is about your grandfather that frustrates you. Don't be angry at *everything* he does. Try to pick out the things that really drive you wild and consider them first.

Does he attempt to make rules for you that you resent? Does he tell you what time you should be in when your parents are already strict enough? If that's the problem, try to imagine your grandfather as a young man. Your age. Running around with his friends. Dating. *Ask him about those days.*

Ask him if he ever stayed out too late. Have him tell you the kinds of things he did as a teenaged boy. *Get to know him as a person, not just as "Grandpa."* He might tell you some stories that you'll find fascinating. He may tell you a few wild stories that will surprise you.

You might be in for another surprise as well. You might start to like Grandpa a little better when you get to know him as a person. If you're really having fun getting to know this "new" guy, get a notebook and start taking notes on his stories. Writing them down is a wonderful tool for learning more about your family and heritage. Besides, it will make Grandpa feel good. Once you meet him halfway and become more than relatives, even *friends,* perhaps you'll find he's easier to deal with. Showing someone a little extra affectionate attention usually changes their attitude for the better. (I know it sure helps mine!)

Perhaps there are other issues that frustrate you. Elderly people sometimes do have habits and physical needs that seem unpleasant to a teenager with few bodily flaws. Does he leave his teeth in a glass in the bathroom at night and gross you out? Then brush yours doubly hard and be glad yours are still in your head!

Seriously, it's tough to handle things like that. Sometimes a sense of humor will be the only thing that gets you through. Talk to your parents about your feelings. They don't want you harboring resentment toward your grandfather. Perhaps they don't even realize how frustrated you've become. Ask them to help you to deal with this.

There's one other thing you can do on a very personal level. Pray for patience with your grandfather. Ask for help in seeing the good in him and the ability to overlook the bad.

This problem with your grandfather is no doubt testing both your patience and your nerves. Don't view that as all negative. Good things can come from bad. You are learning people skills and coping skills that you will use for the rest of your life.

I realize that's not much comfort right now, but you *can* someday look back on this part of your life with no regrets about the way you treated and spoke to your grandfather, and the satisfaction that you did the best you could. These verses from Romans 5:3–5 sum it up: "We also have joy with our troubles because we know that these troubles produce patience. And patience produces character, and character produces hope. And this hope will never disappoint us."

Hang in there. Because of the mature way you've dealt with your problems today, you'll be a smarter, more sensitive adult tomorrow.

*I have a problem similar to Lexi's. My grandpa has Alzheimer's disease and my grandma had a nervous breakdown. Grandpa's getting worse. You can see it happening. He doesn't talk much and forgets a lot. I don't know what my family's going to do when he is not with us. My aunt's got cancer, and my dad has to have an operation on his hip. Everything has been going wrong at the same time. I try to talk to God, but it just doesn't seem like He understands.*

—Valerie, age 12

Everything *does* seem to be going wrong! It would be very easy to grow discouraged in a situation such as yours. You are exactly right in saying that the same sort of thing happened to Lexi Leighton in *Yesterday's Dream*. For a long time she had trouble talking to God, too. Sometimes it feels like God isn't "up there" at all. You might even feel that your prayers are just noise floating through space, but it's not true. Your prayers are finding their way. It's just that there's a cloudy haze of frustration, anger, resentment, and other "junk" preventing you from feeling God's presence. Don't worry. He's there. He won't leave you.

---

## God's presence does not depend on our feelings.

---

Lexi worked through her own haze of negative emotions and feelings to learn a lesson about her grandmother. The lesson she needed to learn was that her grandmother (and your grandfather, too) is part of God's creation. Though old and ill, she was still precious to God.

God loves you (imperfect as you are). He loves your grandfather. Start there. In fact, He loves *everybody* in your family, diseases and all.

Often our feelings (which are changeable and unreliable) get in the way when we're talking to God. When He *feels* far away to you, don't depend on those feelings for a true picture of God and His relationship to you. Feelings change. God doesn't.

*I'm glad that there is a Christian author that really understands how I feel. This may seem weird, but the book* Tomorrow's Promise *really touched me because my grandmother has Alzheimer's disease. We live with her. This book helped me to understand how to deal with it in a Christian-like way. Thank you. Thank you. Thank you!!*

  *If you could find it in your heart,* please *do another one on the subject, or just briefly tell me in a letter how to deal with her because it's* very, very *hard. It's hard not to get upset with this disease. So all I can do is pray.*

—Terri, age 15

Unfortunately there is nothing you can do that will change your grandmother's condition. All you can expect with Alzheimer's is gradual deterioration. That means that things will get worse for her, not better.

The only person you can change in this situation is yourself. Your own mind is a place you can improve. How? It won't be easy. You will have to learn to accept your grandmother just as she is—confused, angry, lost. Due to the disease, your grandmother is becoming more and more like a child in an adult's body. Can you love that child?

It's hard to see adults act in childish ways, but if you can remember that your grandmother is as helpless and defenseless as a young child, then it will be easier for you to understand and deal with her.

Imagine also what must be going on in *her* mind! How difficult it must be to realize in her rational moments that something is radically wrong with her, and that she has no way to stop the progression of the disease or to heal it!

If you can step into her shoes for even a moment and think this way, it will bring you new compassion for your grandmother. When you want to scream at her or are tempted to lose your patience, just remember that she would *never* have chosen this suffering for herself. She doesn't mean to do any harm. If she were able, she would tell you how much she loves you. Now it's your turn to do that for her.

## TWENTY – TWO

## "I Lied to My Mom..."
● ● ● ● ● ● ● ● ●

*I just lied to my mother and I feel guilty. I am not normally the type to lie. I've always been honest. We had these things called assignment and practice sheets and I didn't do them. I owed a bunch of them to my teacher and my mother just found out. She's supposed to read them, sign them, and send them back to school. She was really upset. I lied to her and I am sorry I did.*

—Vanessa, age 11

*I told my mom I was staying overnight at a girlfriend's house and then went out with a guy I'd just met instead. He had some alcohol with him, and we spent the night lying on the grass looking at the stars. Unfortunately, we got caught and now I'm grounded forever.*

—Laurel, age 15

Lying is one of those things that occasionally *seems* like a good idea, but never is. Sometimes telling the truth seems so difficult that lying appears to be the only answer.

WRONG!

I learned as a child that lying never helps and usually makes whatever mess you're in much, much worse. The minute you tell a lie, you set yourself up to tell even *more* lies. You know how it happens: To make the first lie seem true you add a little to it and before you know it, you've got a whole mouthful of lies to keep straight. Then you really get into trouble because you *forget* exactly how you worded that first little lie. Pretty soon you are all tangled up in that "web of deceit." It's a web, all right, just like a spider web. You're all caught up in your lies waiting for the spider (Mom, Dad, or perhaps a teacher or friend) to notice that you're hanging there, snarled up in your own fibs.

## The worst consequence of lying to your parents is destroying their trust in you.

Lying feels lousy. It doesn't even roll off your tongue like the truth does. The words feel foreign and unfamiliar—or at least they should. If lying doesn't feel good to you, be glad. That means your conscience is working, telling you that you've gone too far.

I don't have much tolerance for lying at my house. We've always told our daughters that if they did something wrong they should "fess up" immediately. We've assured them that, although they may get in trouble for what they've done, the punishment will be *nothing* like what will happen if we catch them in a lie.

Actually, the worst thing that can happen to you when you lie to your parents is that you can lose their trust. At first that doesn't sound like such a big deal. Losing your parents' trust sounds easier than being grounded, but it's not.

Parents give their children the *gift* of trust. When I give them that gift I assume that they will not disappoint me. That means that when they are away from me (on a date, at school, working) I am confident that they are fulfilling their responsibilities, being good representatives of our family, doing what they should. If they goof up and do something our family does not approve of (that might include smoking, drinking, stealing, being in someone's home without permission, etc.), and they *admit* to us they've made a bad choice, they will be reprimanded or punished in a manner that fits the "crime."

BUT, if they lie to us or try to cover up the behavior, that's when things get sticky. You see, suddenly I feel I can *never* trust them to behave in a mature, acceptable manner. I no longer feel that they are responsible, mature individuals when they are away from me. *I no longer feel that they can be trusted.*

And what does that mean? At our house, it means that privileges that are the right of mature teens are taken away. It would probably mean having to be in at an earlier hour or being grounded, less spending money, revoking permission to drive the car, and, more importantly, it means that I no longer view that child in the same manner. I don't feel I can count on them anymore. That's a tragedy for me and a disaster for them.

If you've lied to your parents about things such as attending unsupervised parties, seeing boys without permission, telling your parents you'll be one place and actually going to another, and they've caught you in the lie, your life will change, and it should.

Suddenly, when you ask to go out, your parent will wonder, "Why? What kind of trouble is she planning to get into now? Which friend is she *really* intending to see? Are alcohol, cigarettes, or boys going to be involved? Just what is she up to? Maybe she'd just better stay home. . . ."

You can see how questions like that running through a parent's brain would make them less likely to give you permission to leave the house! Once trust is gone between a parent and child, it takes a long, long time to rebuild it.

Two or three blatant lies may ruin your "truth record" for two or three years! When a parent cannot trust a child to do what he says he will do, that parent is unlikely to allow him to do much of anything that is unsupervised or unchaperoned.

It should be coming clear that *how your parents treat you is in part your own choice.* Responsibility, maturity, and honesty will get you trust, respect, and a measure of independence. Lying produces suspicion, disappointment, and restrictions. Is that lie worth it? I don't think so.

There is some good news in all of this, however. If you've been caught lying, there is a light at the end of the tunnel. Even though your earthly parents are going to need proof by your behavior that you aren't going to lie again, your heavenly Father is willing to "wipe the slate clean" and let you start over with Him if you confess your sin and ask His forgiveness.

God is an expert on liars, cheaters, and thieves. He set up His entire heavenly plan for people like that—for people like us. He's just waiting to forgive us when we stumble if only we'll come to Him and tell Him about it! (See how much He's like your earthly parents?) He wants you to confess what you've done wrong. He wants you to repent, or turn away from whatever it was that got you into trouble in the first place. And, He wants you to accept and believe in His forgiveness.

"I did not come to invite good people. I came to invite sinners" (Matthew 9:13).

First of all—*Quit Lying!* Begin immediately to rebuild the trust you've broken with your parents. Then mend the relationship you have with God. Admit you've been wrong. Ask His forgiveness. Ask Him to help you not to make the same mistake again. God is great at giving out fresh starts to people who've goofed things up.

*I like this guy who is four years older than me. He is nineteen and I am fifteen. My mother decided he was too old for me. I tried to talk to her. She just wouldn't listen. She told me not to see him anymore. We've gone out three times since then. I feel guilty about it because my mother and I have always been so close. I've never intentionally gone against anything she's told me. I'm also a Christian and I should honor my mother. But I like him so much . . . he's kissed me. It made it harder for me to break it off. I don't know if I can! I tried praying about it, but I'm still confused. I think my mother is being closed-minded. She's never even met him or heard of him before I said his name to her. I just don't understand why she's being this way. I know going behind her back is wrong, but I really like him. I need good advice. Soon.*

—Mindy, age 15

Whoa! Stop and reread this letter. Think about it. Do you realize what you are doing? Lying. Sneaking out on dates with an older guy? Going against your conscience. Ruining a perfectly good relationship with your mom. Is this guy *worth* it? Probably not.

I understand why you're attracted to this guy. He's older (a better "catch," someone more interesting than those goofy, immature guys at school). He's probably a good kisser because he's had a few more years experience. He's forbidden fruit. (Didn't God tell Eve to leave that apple alone in the Garden of Eden? Could she? Not until after it had gotten her into deep trouble!) He's no doubt cute, charming, and fun.

He's also already out of high school and apparently unable to find a girlfriend his own age. A relationship between a man and a woman who is four years younger isn't significant if both people are in their thirties or forties. It *is* significant at fifteen and nineteen.

There's one more thing about this situation that I consider the creepiest aspect of all. Apparently this guy is willing to let you lie to your mom about him! If he is willing to let you sneak out of your house to date him on the sly, he's not worth bothering with. If he's man enough to come to the house, meet your parents, and let them get to know him and decide about him for themselves, then, at least you could respect him.

---

**On a date, always remember: *You* are in charge of your life. The only power your date holds over you is the power *you've* given him.**

---

You also mentioned that since he's kissed you, you didn't know if you'd be able to break off the relationship. *Of course you can!* You are in charge of your life, not this guy! He doesn't have any magical power over you. The only power he holds over you is the power *you've* given him. You can break up whenever you choose. Don't fool yourself into thinking otherwise.

Remember that your mother is only trying to protect you. She doesn't want to see you hurt, but you are already on a misguided path if you are deceiving her by sneaking out behind her back. There was a reason that God said in Proverbs 6:20–23, "My son (that includes daughters too), keep your father's commands. *Don't forget your mother's teaching.* Remember their words forever. . . . They will guide you when you walk. They will guard you while you sleep. They will speak to you when you are awake. Their commands are like a lamp. Their teaching is like a light. And the correction that comes from them helps you have life."

You are trying to be independent from your parents. That's normal and natural for teenagers. But in this search for independence, don't ignore what your parents are trying to teach you or reject the advice they have to give to you. Now is the time when you *want* them around the least and yet *need* them most. It's your parents' responsibility to protect you. That's all your mom is doing. She's a mom. It's her job.

You say that you have a close relationship with your mother. Talk to her. Be honest and forthright. Tell her how you feel. Tell her that you'd like her to listen to you with an open mind. Sometimes it is hard for parents to see a teen's side of things, but lovingly encourage her to try. Ask for her insight. She was a teenager once, too, you know. (When dinosaurs roamed the earth, right?)

Perhaps this can be a springboard for a new, deeper relationship between the two of you.

I have a sixteen-year-old. Often I see so clearly what is right for her that I *order* her to do things. That makes her mad! We moms have things to learn too, you know! I work hard at honest, open communication with her—and she must do the same for me. Sometimes (if I feel she is in real danger of hurting herself physically, emotionally, or spiritually) I have to tell her, "You must listen to me because I'm the adult and I'm responsible for you." Other times we can settle an issue in a manner that satisfies us both. I realize that this doesn't sound easy or fun, but, in this instance, it is the right thing to do. Most of all, be grateful that you have a mother who loves you so!

Next time you are tempted to lie, think of this verse. "The Lord hates those who tell lies. But he is pleased with those who do what they promise" (Proverbs 12:22).

## TWENTY – THREE

# "My Father Is a Cold Man..."

• • • • • • • • •

*My father believes that showing emotion is wrong, a little like a sin. My brothers and sisters and I aren't allowed to show our emotions either. After thirteen years of his stern, strict, and angry personality, all my feelings are ready to burst out.*

*My father never really spends time with me or anyone else. Instead, he spends all of his time in front of the TV or at work. I am ready to tell him just what I think of him, but I don't want to. I will get into so much trouble and he will be very, very hurt.*

*I told God all of this, but I need a human person to talk to. I can't tell my mother because she loves my father and she would be hurt.*

*Do you know who I should talk to? I've run out of people. I know you will probably suggest my pastor. He won't work. We're new in town and I don't know him very well.*

*—Lisa, age 13*

*I have no major problems except my dad. He works a lot and he comes home late at night. He's always mad when he comes home. And he doesn't ever get excited anymore. The sparkle has left his eyes. Will you pray for him? Please!*

—Elizabeth, age 13

Does this sound like your dad? "A happy heart is like good medicine. But a broken spirit drains your strength" (Proverbs 17:22). Is his spirit broken and his strength drained?

Fathers (and mothers) are under a lot of pressure these days. They have financial responsibilities for their families, concerns about the recession, the threat of layoffs, and the cutting of government programs that may affect them. They also have the normal run-of-the-mill hassles that come with being in the work force and raising a family. It's not surprising that people are tense and angry sometimes, but when it begins to affect the family, something needs to be done.

If you are ready to explode with pent-up hostility and frustration, *you need to talk this out*!

Try talking to your mom. You aren't giving her enough credit when you say that you don't dare tell her how you feel about your dad because she would be hurt. She loves you too, you know! She's the one who can help you work this out (or, if she can't, she knows how to find people who will help you).

Here's a suggestion. Don't just run up to her and blurt out all your anger and frustration. *Plan what you are going to say. Think it through carefully. Take notes if you have to!* Organize your thoughts so that when you approach this subject you are calm and confident. Sometimes, if I have a very important telephone call to make and I want to get everything just right, I make a list of all that I want to say. I plan the questions I will ask and the points I want to make.

When something is very important to you, don't leave things up to chance. Take control of your own life and your own words. If you can't speak of this without exploding, write out your thoughts on paper and hand it to her.

If you absolutely can't get the words out (and I hope you can, because I'm sure your mother loves you very much and wants to help you), then go to your school counselor. You do need to discuss this with someone. You don't want to end up like a mini-volcano, erupting tears and emotions all over the place.

And when you are dealing with your dad, think of this verse: "Worry makes a person feel as if he is carrying a heavy load. But a kind word cheers up a person" (Proverbs 12:25). You can be the one who cheers him up with that kind word. It might not work at first, but don't give up. I'm certain that parents can *never* hear too many kind, cheerful, loving words from their children! We're like sponges, soaking up all the sweetness you can offer us.

## TWENTY – FOUR

## "My Mom Died..."

● ● ● ● ● ● ● ● ●

*My relatives have been dropping dead like flies in the last couple of years.*

—Eileen, age 13

*I've read your whole series and often find myself in similar situations.* Yesterday's Dreams *really got to me. My mom passed away recently.*

—Jaclyn, age 16

*Here's some dumb junk about me:*
*Name: Bobbie Jo*
*B-day: September 17*
*Grade: 5th*
*Age: 11*
*Something about me: My face is ugly and my attitude stinks.*
*Hardest, but most recent thing in my life: My mom went to be with the Lord on Tuesday. Yeah, my mom had cancer for four years and she died on Tuesday.*

—Bobbie Jo, age 11

The first thing I noticed about your letter was the way you threw that information about the death of your mother into that list of "dumb junk about me." I've been thinking about that a lot and it's been troubling me. Do you want to know why? Because I think you're trying to be tough and nonchalant (that means not flustered or upset) about something that's so important to you that you don't want to deal with it.

Sometimes, when something very sad or bad or embarrassing happens to a person, she tries to deal with it by pretending it didn't happen or that it didn't really bother her. That works for a little while, but not for long.

---

## The death of a parent is one of the most traumatic things that can happen to a child of any age.

---

You feel sad, angry, abandoned, helpless, and frightened all at the same time. What's more, there's nothing you can do to bring that parent back to be with you again.

Don't try to be too tough or act too self-controlled. No one expects you to be strong right now. Give yourself the chance to grieve.

What does that mean, exactly?

*Grieving.* It's a word that even sounds sad, but it is the beginning of the healing process. It's the first step you must take. The Bible gives you permission to be sad and mournful over the death of your mother. It also reminds you that, because you are Christians, there is good news even in death. "Brothers, we want you to know about those who have died. We do not want you to be sad as others who have no hope. We believe that Jesus died and that he rose again. So, because of Jesus, God will bring together with Jesus those who have died" (1 Thessalonians 4:13–14).

This verse says you can be sad about those who have died, but you don't have to be as sad as the people who don't believe that Jesus died and rose again! You know that you will be seeing them again!

Go ahead. Cry. Jesus did. The shortest verse in the Bible

116

is "Jesus cried" (John 11:35). He'll understand your tears.

There's a tiny book titled *Good Grief*, by Granger E. Westberg, that simply explains all those feelings you are having right now and all the stages you will probably go through before you can really accept your mother's death. It might help your entire family to read it.

People sometimes walk around for a long time in a state of shock before they can accept with their heart as well as their head that someone they love is gone. They may even refuse to let themselves cry.

Where is God at a time like this? You might even wonder if He's abandoned you completely. Or maybe you're doubting that He even exists. If He did, wouldn't He have healed your mother? Those questions aren't evil or unnatural. In fact, when Jesus was dying on the cross, even *He* began to wonder if God had forgotten about Him. He cried, "My God, my God, why have you left me alone?" (Matthew 27:46). If *Jesus* once felt abandoned by God, it's no wonder that you might feel the same way.

But God hasn't abandoned you. He hasn't moved away.

Christians have several things working in their favor. First of all, we view death differently from those who don't believe in Christ. We don't believe that death is permanent. We believe that there is another, far better life after this one. This is all summed up in my very favorite verses in the Bible—"Everyone who believes in him can have eternal life. For God loved the world so much that he gave his only son. God gave his son so that whoever believes in him may not be lost, but have eternal life" (John 3:15–16).

Not only does the Bible talk about eternal life, it talks about *where* we'll be—in Jesus' house, with Him. He says, "There are many rooms in my Father's house. I would not tell you this if it were not true. I am going there to prepare a place for you" (John 14:2). That doesn't sound so bad, does it? Staying with Jesus at His place? Christians can count on going to Jesus' place when they die. After all, Jesus has said we would and *He does not tell lies.*

Sometimes, even if we're sure that our loved one has gone to heaven, we still have trouble back here on earth.

It's that *guilt* thing. Those unkind or impatient words we wish we could take back. The time you didn't spend with your grandpa or grandma. The fun you made of them behind their backs. The things you wished you'd said or done. You know—guilt. This feeling of guilt is miserable and unproductive. What's more, it can stop the healing process.

That's heavy-duty stuff, because you can't go back and undo the damage you feel you've done—at least not by yourself. Here's where Christians have that second advantage. We can go to God and ask Him to help us with our guilt, the "I should haves," and the "I wish I hadn'ts."

He's perfectly willing to forgive you for those things you feel badly about. God knows us better than we know ourselves and He's *still* willing to forgive us. "If we say we have no sin, we are fooling ourselves, and the truth is not in us. But if we confess our sins, he will forgive our sins. We can trust God. He does what is right. He will make us clean from all the wrongs we have done" (1 John 1:8–9). Neat, huh? This gives us permission to forgive ourselves. *What a relief!*

*To my friend Judy Baer,*

*My aunt takes care of my brother, my sister, and me. My mom and dad died. My mom died of an overdose of heroin and my dad died in a car accident. He was drunk and on drugs. My dad died a week before my mom! I'm not real sad because my mom is in heaven. What scares me is that I don't know where my dad went.*

—Ingrid, age 11

I understand your fear. When I was a child, I always used to worry when I heard that someone had died. "Did they believe in God?" I'd wonder. "Where are they now? What has happened to their soul?"

The most joyous funeral I ever attended was for a woman who possessed a deep faith all her life. I didn't have to worry for even a moment. I *knew* where she was and that she was happy now. The only tears anyone shed were for themselves because they would miss her.

Unfortunately, you don't have that feeling about your dad's death. Just remember that your dad's eternity is in God's hands now. And that's good news because *God is in the business of forgiving people!* Your dad is God's responsibility now. He is a loving, forgiving God. His loving justice is fair and righteous. He will do what is right. Turn your concern over to Him. Leave God in charge.

*In* Yesterday's Dream *I knew exactly how Lexi was feeling . . . especially the "Why Me?" question when her grandpa died. I recently lost my grandfather and he was kind and loving, fun, and caring too.*

—Katherine, age 11

*Reading your book has helped me a lot. I had a lot of mixed feelings for God. I blamed Him for my dad's death. I still wonder if He is real.*

—Katie, age 14

Is God real? Good question. You have the right to ask. The fact is, I *know* He is.

Sometimes I compare God to electricity or computers. I'm not much of an electrician or a computer whiz, but I know that if I flip on the light switch in my office, I get light. I also know that if I punch the keys on my computer in the right sequence, I get a menu up on the screen that allows me to write. I can't *see* electricity or understand the software that makes my computer compute, but I *know* it works. It works for me every single day. I have *faith* that it will work for me tomorrow.

Sometimes, if the electricity goes out, my lights won't light and my computer won't compute, but I know that it's only a temporary disturbance in the atmosphere around me. It doesn't mean that electricity doesn't exist. It only means I'm getting a little interference.

God is like that. He's there, waiting to be discovered, willing to work for you. He doesn't change. He's always the same.

## Doubting God's existence doesn't make Him go away. That doubt is a temporary disturbance in your atmosphere!

Having faith in something you can't see, touch, or even understand is tough. So tough, in fact, that it's impossible for us to do it by ourselves. *God even has to give us the faith it takes to believe in Him!* "You are saved by grace, and you got that grace by believing. You did not save yourselves. It was a gift from God" (Ephesians 2:8).

Try this. Say, "Dear God, I'm having trouble believing in you right now. My faith is so little and weak that it practically doesn't exist. Please give me the faith I need to believe in you! Please show me who you are."

Sometimes God answers our prayers and we don't even hear Him because we aren't really expecting an answer. Be open to Him. Expect an answer. Then you'll be ready when it comes.

Faith is a difficult thing to explain. A good word to describe faith is "nebulous." That means it is shapeless, hazy, and hard to understand—until, of course, you've experienced it. "Faith means being sure of the things we hope for. And faith means knowing that something is real even if we do not see it" (Hebrews 11:1).

All Christians have to live this way: "We live by what we believe, not by what we can see" (2 Corinthians 5:7).

So, next time you flip on a light switch, think about God. He's there, just like the current running to that switch. And even though you can't see Him or truly understand Him, believe in Him. Once you begin to experience God's power and light, you'll never want to go back to the darkness of life without Him.

*There is so much that has happened in my life. My mother died and I was put in a foster home. Now I have my new parents. They are very strong Christians. Sometimes I feel depressed and your books help me through it. Thanks.*

—Michelle, age 14

*Books #9 and #10 mean a lot to me. My dad died and I felt the same way Lexi did.*

—Penny, age 11

*My grandmother died of Alzheimer's disease. Our family didn't take care of Grandma, because we couldn't do it. We put her in a nursing home. The last time I saw her was last summer. She died a week later. I'd always hated my grandmother, as if she had done something wrong by getting sick. I never realized that I'd blamed her for my mistakes until I read your book. Now I have a deeper understanding of the feelings that were going on inside of me. I talked to the Lord about this, and I just wanted you to know that your book has changed my life.*

—Trisha, age 16

*I have just finished the book* Tomorrow's Promise. *This book has given me a lot to think about, which is probably why I am writing this letter at two in the morning! This book has brought back a lot of hurt and frustration that I harbored within me since my grandfather's death. Because of this I have doubted myself as a Christian, and have fallen away from God. I guess I just realized that going through the motions just isn't good enough.*

—Vickie, age 14

At times we all start "going through the motions" of life for one reason or another. Fortunately, we have a God who is willing to let us start over with a clean slate when this happens. We're forgiven. Perfect in His sight. A new creation. You can't get any better than that!

One of my favorite Bible verses is Psalm 103:12, "He has taken our sins away from us as far as the east is from west."

Do you know how *far* that is? If you send two rockets into space, one going east, the other west, will they ever meet? No. They will travel in two entirely different directions through the universe forever and ever. That's pretty far!

That's how far away God puts our sins when He forgives us. He not only forgives, but He forgets. That's the part I like best. Even if I forgive someone for hurting me, when I see that person, I can still remember what she did to me. God doesn't even *remember* our sin once He has forgiven us. He looks at us and sees us as brand new and without sin.

Therefore, you can stop "going through the motions" and start fresh with God. It's a gift like no other. Take it. Enjoy it.

## TWENTY – FIVE

# "It's Hard to Be a Pastor's (Lawyer's, Doctor's, *Anybody's*) Kid!"

● ● ● ● ● ● ● ●

*Some problems in your books have happened to me, my family, and my friends. It's hard for me to cope because my dad's a pastor. Everybody thinks I have to be a perfect angel and set a good example, but I'm just human and make mistakes. I don't advertise my religion or keep it a secret. Your books help me in many areas. My dad's always gone, my mom works uptown, and when they are home they are barely ever in a good mood. My dad is just human, too.*

—Louise, age 13

I know what you're saying. It's tough to be a pastor's kid. You feel as though you have a higher set of standards than "ordinary" kids. What's more, you have an entire congregation full of observers who take a special interest in you. That's fine if you're doing something wonderful, but if you goof up, it's not so great.

Frankly, it's not that easy being *anyone's* kid. There are always jealousies, unreasonable expectations, and troubles at home that keep life from being perfect. But all anyone can expect of you is that you *do the best you can.*

We are all human. We get tired. We get cranky. Our hormones zip up and down and make us moody. But, in spite of this, if we at least try to be cheerful, considerate, dependable, and hard-working, then that will be good enough.

Often people have a tendency to put a pastor and his family on a pedestal, thinking they are better and have more faith and wisdom than the rest of us. That's a heavy burden, especially since the Bible says, "*All people* have sinned . . ." (Romans 3:23).

Just keep your position in perspective. Grin and bear it. (Smiling is always a much better option than frowning when you can't do anything about your circumstances anyway!)

---

**You can't be perfect, but you are already a very special person, one of a kind.**

---

## TWENTY – SIX

## "Someone I Love is Mentally Ill . . ."

● ● ● ● ● ● ● ● ●

*So many times I have been in situations like Lexi's. I have just finished reading books #9 and #10, and I just wanted to say thank you!*

*My family is going through a similar situation with a very unpredictable aunt. She does not have Alzheimer's but she is mentally ill. She thinks people are trying to kill her. It is hard to show someone like that you love them.*

*I can relate to Lexi in so many ways. She encourages me and I just wanted to say . . . THANK YOU.*

—Renee, age 15

I wish I had an easy answer for you, but there isn't one. You have very little control over your aunt's behavior. Actually, the only person you have control over is yourself. Therefore, to get through this difficult time, you will have to make some decisions about how you will treat this situation.

First, you could try to ignore it, but I don't think that's either wise or possible. Your entire family is in turmoil

**125**

right now, and pretending there's nothing wrong is both unrealistic and unproductive.

You could also worry about your aunt's condition until you begin to wonder about your own sanity. That, of course, would be a complete waste of time and energy.

The third and most productive idea is to accept the situation and make the best of it.

Your aunt is ill. Only trained professionals can help her through this. Trust the adults around you to see that she gets the care she needs. The thing you can do best is pray for her. Remember, God loves your aunt. He is concerned for her well-being. "The Lord does not ignore the one who is in trouble. He doesn't hide from him. He listens when the one in trouble calls out to him" (Psalm 22:24). See? Already you are not alone in this.

It's hard not to be embarrassed or ashamed when someone you love is doing strange, unpredictable things, but you must try to remember that mental illness is an *illness*. Your aunt did not choose to be ill. She needs medical help just as much as she would if she had cancer or a broken leg. Don't let her strange behavior make you love her any less.

# PART II

# Siblings

● ● ● ● ● ● ● ● ●

*"Whoever loves a brother or sister lives in the light,
and in such a person there is no cause for stumbling."*

1 JOHN 2:10

# INTRODUCTION

Parents don't cause the only problems in a teenager's family life. Brothers and sisters can produce an entirely different set of headaches.

I receive surprisingly few letters about problems with siblings. I hope this means that most families function without too much stress and strain, but somehow I doubt that's the case. As the mother of two, I often see the love-hate relationship between my own daughters. A sister can be a best friend and a worst enemy—all within the space of five minutes.

My girls can be enjoying (and I choose the word "enjoying" because I do believe that they relish their arguments) a riproaring disagreement, but when I step in to scold one of them, suddenly, magically, *I'm* the bad guy. The two, who were battling with such fury only seconds before, are suddenly defending each other against their big, bad mom.

When I hear the sounds of conflict, I go to the source, where the girls are faced off, glaring at each other. The conversation might go something like this:

"You didn't ask me if you could wear that! I wanted to wear it today!" says Daughter Number One.

"It was in the clothes hamper. You couldn't have wanted it," claims Daughter Number Two.

"Did too!"

"Did not!"

"What's going on in here? Why are you wearing your sister's clothes? Haven't we discussed this before?" (That's me talking, if you couldn't already tell.)

"Mother! She wasn't doing anything wrong." (That's Daughter Number One, the one whose voice I could hear over the whine of the vacuum cleaner and the roar of the dishwasher.)

"Then what is all the yelling about?" I ask. "And why were you in her closet?"

"You wouldn't understand."

"Why not? I have a college degree." (I sometimes get sarcastic when the conversation gets too ridiculous.)

"You're an only child."

"Yeah. You don't know what it's like." (That's Daughter Number Two. The one who was furious with her sister only a moment ago.)

"Try me. I have a good imagination."

"Sisters always talk like that. We weren't arguing. We were just . . . discussing. She took my blouse but she's trading me a pair of shoes for it."

"I thought you were fighting over something in the dirty clothes hamper."

"We weren't fighting!"

"I wouldn't talk that way to my worst enemy. And if you've got this all worked out, why were you yelling?"

"Oh, motherrr . . ." they chime together.

Suddenly, I'm on the outside looking in and they are defending each other against *me*. Now I'm the bad guy! I try not to smile. I envy that exclusive club of which I am not a part. After all, I never had a sister. . . .

Does any of this sound familiar? Unless you are an only child, I'm sure it does. Conflict, interpersonal relationships, learning to share and to sacrifice—it's all part of what a family is about. A family is the cocoon where we learn about life. Family life—its ups and downs, the support, the compromises, the joys, the disappointments—prepares us for life in the "real world." It's a safe place to try out the many facets of your personality (even the nasty ones) and still be confident you will be loved. Sisters and brothers (even the most irritating ones) can help you learn how to deal with others. There are lessons to be learned that will last your entire life.

If your family unit is working well, life can be good. Divorce, remarriage, and the resulting blended families, however, can also make relationships more complicated than ever before. . . .

## TWENTY – SEVEN

# "My Father Likes My Brother More Than He Does Me..."

● ● ● ● ● ● ● ● ●

*The characters in Cedar River Daydreams have really inspired me, especially Alexis Leighton. Her prayers and thoughts have made me think about my own life. I now realize how far apart from God I really am. This may be a result of my relationship with my father, which isn't that great. We get into lots of arguments, especially since my brother was born. My father favors him over me no matter what. This is no excuse for my relationship with God, but it sure would be easier if my relationship with my earthly father was better. I know it is wrong, but sometimes I get jealous and angry at my brother because he gets anything he wants. If you can, please give me some suggestions that might help me to trust God more, especially in this area of my life.*

—Tessa, age 15

You never mentioned your mom. Where is she while this is going on? It sounds as though you need someone to "intercede" for you—someone who can speak on your behalf and try to reconcile the differences between you and your father. If your mom could help you, talk to her. It's easy to get upset when you feel you aren't being treated fairly. Maybe you'll have to talk to your dad yourself. Have you tried that, or does it seem too scary? He might not even realize what is happening. You should give him the opportunity to change things.

---

## When relationships have deteriorated too much, it is often difficult to "put them back together" without help.

---

Is it possible that you are a little bit jealous of your brother?

It's easy to be jealous, but it leaves you feeling miserable and left out. You'll be happier if you can get rid of that emotion.

Perhaps your father believes he's treating you special each in your own way, according to your own personalities. He might need a "nudge" to remind him that you'd like to play catch or go fishing just as your brother does.

Your brother has never had your life experiences, so it is quite impossible for him to understand your troubled relationship with your father. I'm not sure it's even worth trying to explain it to him. What seems like great injustices to you might seem petty and insignificant to him.

Even though it's difficult, try not to blame your brother for the favoritism your father shows. After all, if you begin to resent both of them, you will not only damage the relationship with your father but the one with your brother as well. There's no use injuring a relationship that would otherwise last a lifetime.

You need to talk to someone about your feelings. It's not good to keep resentment and frustrations inside. The Bible tells you this: "Peace of mind means a healthy body. Jealousy will rot your bones" (Proverbs 14:30).

Sounds pretty gross, doesn't it? But jealousy and unhappiness can shrivel a person inside. You must take care of your spiritual as well as your physical self.

It is clear from your letter that you are struggling with not only family relationships but with your own faith as well. You would benefit from a Bible study or fellowship group, which could give you new insights and answer the questions you have about your faith. Check it out at church. Get into Sunday school again if you've left.

Is there a trusted pastor you could talk to? A youth group you could join? When I was fifteen, I worked through several Bible studies aimed at teens. They can be done on your own and be of personal benefit. Most of all, remember that God is only a prayer away from you.

*I have problems. I can't talk to my mom about them because it would just make her angry, so I hope you can give me some advice. My mom treats my brother better than me! I think it's because he was born first. My brother will hit me and I'll tell my mom but she takes his side instead of mine. She always says the same thing. "He has problems and you always tell when he's just goofing off. You two fight over the stupidest things." My brother lies and says that I hit him first. I don't understand why she never believes me! My parents are divorced and they are both remarried. Now I have five stepbrothers and one real brother. I'm the only girl! I love my parents, but it seems as if my mom cares more about my brother than me!*

—Annette, age 11

I think that all children who have brothers and sisters have at some time or another felt the way you're feeling right now. Many years ago there was a comedy team of two brothers who based all their jokes on the complaint "Mom always liked you best!" One brother acted downtrodden and rejected, the other confident and secure. If two grown men could *earn a living* complaining that their mom played favorites, then you know that the feeling is very common.

From your description, it sounds as though your mom has had a lot on her mind—including a divorce and seven children. She's probably tired and impatient more than she'd like to be, and your problems with your brother may not seem very significant to her. That doesn't mean they are unimportant, however.

I realize that you don't feel you can talk to your mom

about this, but she is *exactly* the person you must talk to. Here's some advice: Don't try to talk to her just after she's told you that "you two fight over the stupidest things." Wait until sometime when the household is peaceful and she's in a good mood. Then curl up next to her on the couch and ask her if you can talk to her about something that's been worrying you. Tell her what you've been concerned about. Ask her to help you feel better about yourself and your place in the family. That's what moms are for.

You also hinted that your brother might have "problems" that you didn't describe in your letter. If he has learning disabilities or health problems, your mom might, without really thinking about it, baby him a little more, and you are picking up on that. If that's the case, then you should discuss that too. Sometimes, because your mother is so worried about your brother, she might choose his side over yours. Perhaps just pointing this out will be enough to make a difference.

Moms aren't perfect either, but in most cases they do try to do their best for their children. Put some trust in yours and see what happens.

## TWENTY EIGHT

## "My Sister Is _____" (Bossy/ Selfish/ Rude—You Fill In the Blank!)

● ● ● ● ● ● ● ● ●

*I like your book,* The Intruder, *because many people have that problem. I had a stepsister who was rude too.*

—Jessica, age 10

I don't think it's just *step*sisters who can be bossy, selfish, or rude. At one time or another, any sister can display one or more of those characteristics. Sometimes all within the space of a few seconds! In fact, I've noticed that girls are often *more* rude or bossy to their sisters than they are to anyone else.

Believe it or not, there's a reason for this. Sisters are often less careful of their sibling's feelings because *they aren't afraid of losing their love.* If you were rude or unpleasant to a friend, that person might quickly become an ex-friend. You can never become an ex-sister. Still, that's no reason for treating someone in your family badly. The people in your family are the ones who will be with you and stand by you for the rest of your life. Take care of them!

There's an old, old saying that says, "Treat your friends

like family and your family like friends." That's good advice. When friends visit, you should try to make them feel like they are completely welcome, free to relax and enjoy your home. On the other hand, you should make sure your family is treated with the courtesy and respect you would give to people you don't know very well but would like to get to know better. (Imagine if you always smiled pleasantly at your sister and asked her how she was doing when you met her in the hall. She might freak out, but she'd probably feel special!)

Another thing you must keep in mind is that no two people are alike. Even sisters. They might have totally different personalities, tastes, and dispositions. That's okay.

---

## When you live in the same house with someone who is your total opposite, you might have to work at keeping it peaceful.

---

There are even sisters in the Bible who were completely unalike in disposition. (See, you aren't so very different after all!)

While Jesus and His followers were traveling, Jesus went into a town. A woman named Martha let Jesus stay at her house. While Martha's sister Mary sat at Jesus' feet listening to Him teach, Martha became angry because she had so much work to do. She said, "Lord, don't you care that my sister has left me alone to do all the work? Tell her to help me!"

But the Lord answered her, "Martha, Martha, you are getting worried and upset about too many things. Only one thing is important. Mary has chosen the right thing, and it will never be taken away from her" (Luke 10:38–42).

Can you see the difference between the two sisters? Martha was a workaholic, worried about getting her work done. After all, they had company—Jesus! Mary, on the other hand, didn't feel a bit guilty about leaving her chores until later. She wanted to sit by Jesus and hear what He had to say. Her priorities and actions were entirely different from those of her sister.

Does this make Martha bad and Mary good? Of course not. Jesus didn't think that, either. All He did was encourage Martha to worry a little less about her household chores and take time to spend with Him. Martha's personality was no doubt different than Mary's, and she needed to be settled down a little before she remembered what was really important about Jesus' visit. (It wasn't how clean her house was or how delicious her meal. It was the time they spent together.)

If two sisters like Martha and Mary made it into the Bible and were disagreeing, do you actually think you'll be able to avoid disagreement in your own family?

Being at odds with a *stepsister* is an even more special situation because other things that have nothing to do with you may be going on.

She may be bossy or rude because she feels insecure or resentful. After all, your presence changes *her* family as well as yours. Maybe she isn't so sure her mom or dad loves her quite as much as she or he did before the new marriage. Perhaps she feels you've intruded on her territory. After all, she had one parent all to herself before. Now she has to share.

Once you understand that your stepsister has some problems and worries, too, it might be easier for you to be a little kinder, a little more patient, a little more loving.

In my book, *The Intruder,* Lexi Leighton has to learn to live with Amanda, a foster child who is jealous of Lexi's relationship with her mom and dad. Amanda resents the fact that Lexi is a "birth" child. Most importantly of all, she doesn't realize that *moms and dads actually do have enough love to go around*!

Love is funny that way. The more of it you are willing to give away, the more you have to give. Loving and caring for someone is a wonderful feeling. The more you experience it, the more of it you'll want to experience! Try it. See how it works.

One more suggestion—When that sister or stepsister is being particularly nasty, don't be nasty right back. In Exodus 21:24, it's called punishing "eye for eye, tooth for tooth."

*Dear Judy,*

Yuk! If your sister poked your eye out, that means you'd poke hers out as punishment. We'd all be a blind, bloody mess if we did that. Jesus gives us some other advice about how to handle people who've done something bad to you.

" 'Lord, when my brother sins against me, how many times must I forgive him? Should I forgive him as many as 7 times?' Jesus answered, 'I tell you, you must forgive him more than 7 times. You must forgive him even if he does wrong to you 77 times' " (Matthew 18:21–22).

If you follow that advice, and if you have spats like I suspect *most* sisters have, there should be a whole lot of forgiving going on!

## TWENTY – NINE

## "My Parents Take In Foster Children..."

●　●　●　●　●　●　●　●　●

*My parents have taken foster children. Most people think that the foster child is the only one with problems, but I have problems, too. Ever since our newest foster child (we've had four) came to stay with us, I've had more problems than ever because she does stuff like take money from my wallet, and say that she loves my own mom more than I do.*

　　　　　　　　　　　　　　　　—Jamie, age 14

Never having been a foster child, I can only guess at what it must be like. Perhaps you, too, should try to imagine what it would feel like to be moved into a family that's not your own, knowing that for one reason or another you could not stay in your own home.

The first thing I'd feel is *insecure*. I'd be afraid that someone in the house wouldn't like me, that I'd be moved again, that I would be rejected by my new family, too. I'd be particularly worried about the kids in my new family. After all, they were there first. They've been the recipients of all the foster mom and dad's love and concern up until now. My question would be, "Will there be any love left for me?" Do you think that's why your foster sister says she loves your mom so much? Because she so desperately wants your mom to love her back?

I'd probably feel a little *resentful* too. I'd wish that my life had been as easy as that of the teenagers in my new family. It would seem that they don't even know what trouble is—at least when compared to mine!

I'd also be *afraid*. I'd probably be afraid of everything— of having to leave, of having to stay, of not being liked. . . . I can think of dozens of things to be afraid of if I had to leave my family and live with a new, strange one.

Perhaps if you try to put yourself in this latest foster child's shoes, you'll be able to understand her more fully. Then you'll be less confused and frustrated by the things she says and does.

I wrote about a foster child in *The Intruder*. She acted very much like the foster child you now have in your home. In that book, Lexi Leighton devised a "Three-Part Plan" to win over the new girl.

*Part I:* Pray. Pray for the help you need to get along with this girl. Matthew 5:44 says, "Love your enemies. Pray for those who hurt you." Give it a try.

*Part II:* Try to make her feel loved and cared for by you. Help her to know that affection will get her further than resentment. This is taking action on your prayers.

*Part III:* Tell your mom and dad how you've been feeling. Ask them to help you work through this. Don't try to do it on your own.

Lexi tried this plan in *The Intruder*. It didn't work perfectly, but it helped. At first, for every step she took forward she took two steps back. Finally, Lexi and Amanda were able to resolve their differences. It might be frustrating and time-consuming, but make the decision to love this foster child even if she acts as though she doesn't want to be loved. You'll feel better and I think she will, too.

## THIRTY

## "I'm a Foster Kid..."

● ● ● ● ● ● ● ●

*I am a foster kid. I have been in and out of foster homes. I have never been in a home like I am in now. In this home I have been shown and taught so much love for myself and others. I also receive a lot of love from my foster parents. I really believe if I hadn't come to live here I wouldn't be alive now. My foster mother told me about the love of God. I have been a Christian for one year. I am very happy. In fact, I have never been this happy in my whole entire life.*

—Lois, age 16

This is the other side of the coin. Foster kids are often children who've been tossed around, unsure of who loves and wants them.

> **It's easier to understand, to forgive, and even to love if you can imagine some of the things a foster child has gone through.**

Sometimes the ones who need love the most behave in

the most unlovable manner. They've already decided to reject you before you have the chance to reject them. What a difference putting Christ in this equation can make! "I give you a new command: Love each other. You must love each other as I have loved you" (John 13:34).

*Can I tell you something? Good. I live in a foster home. I will be adopted soon. My sisters and I were taken from our mom because she used to drink. She was given a list of things to do to get me and my sisters back. She did all the things on the list and then decided to sign the release paper to give us up anyway. I got over the mad part but not the hurt part.*

—Tiffany, age 12

It's hard to get rid of the hurt. You're feeling abandoned, rejected, not good enough. *But it's not true!* You are definitely "good enough." This was your mother's problem, not yours.

It might help you to imagine yourself in your mother's shoes, to understand where she was coming from when she made this decision. Perhaps she felt insecure, unsure she could support you and your sister. Perhaps she was afraid—afraid of the future, afraid of her addiction. Maybe she worried about what would happen if she started drinking again. Unless you can crawl into your mother's mind, you cannot fully understand all that went into her decision. Perhaps she felt that giving you up was not an act of cruelty but of love.

Whatever your mother's reasons, *do not blame yourself.* You are valuable, unique, special. I believe that. You should, too.

## THIRTY – ONE

## "My Sister/Brother Has Down's Syndrome..."

● ● ● ● ● ● ● ● ●

*I really enjoyed your book,* New Girl In Town. *I liked it because it was about a real-life situation. My brother is mentally retarded. When we moved to a new town, I had to explain to everyone about him. When I'm seen with him I get some strange looks, but it doesn't bother me much because I love my brother and I am proud to be his sister.*

—Frances, age 14

*I am thirteen, and I love reading Cedar River Daydreams books, since I often find myself in some of Lexi's situations. I know what it's like to have a younger brother with Down's syndrome, since I have a younger sister who has it. I think having a sister with Down's syndrome has taught me a lot about having patience and understanding people with disabilities more. Most of all, she's shown me love.*

—Terri, age 13

*The past two summers our church has been looking after hand-*

145

*icapped children for a couple of hours once a week. The children are lovely. Ben, in your book, describes them exactly. At first, I was scared in case someone saw me with them, but I soon felt relaxed with them. Have you had any experience with Down's syndrome children?*

—Gail, age 13

*I read your first book of Cedar River Daydreams. I liked it a lot, but when I finished it, I felt guilty. I never did like retarded people. Now I know better.*

—Diana, age 11

*The daycare I go to, they have a handicapped kid named Mike. He is so smart. And cute. Handicapped people should be allowed in public.*

—Jenny, age 10

*Ben seems to be just a doll! A lot of Lexi's problems seem to be real life.*

—Lori, age 13

*In the book when Ben got run over by a car, I cried. It was late at night, but I couldn't stop until I knew Ben was all right.*

—Gina, age 11

*A lot of the problems that Lexi and her friends go through are the problems I go through, too. Like Lexi's little brother Ben, I have an older brother who is handicapped. My brother is autistic. He looks normal but his speech is a little below his age. Some people at school love to tease me about him, but I just ignore them and protect my brother because I love him.*

—Wendy, age 13

*When I get into one of your books, I can't put it down. Some people call me a "bookaholic." I was wondering if you thought that was good.*
*I know a lot of people do treat Down's syndrome people badly,*

*and it doesn't make sense to me. They can talk and understand things. There are two high-school-aged kids at my church. I don't know them well, but I say "hi" to them. Some people even at my church totally ignore them or whisper behind their backs. Why can't people, especially Christians, realize that they are people, too? You taught me more about Down's syndrome than I knew before. Thanks a lot!!*

—Sonya, age 12

*In* New Girl in Town *Minda gets mad at seeing a little retarded boy named Ben. The question is why? Why do people think differently about retarded people? In the story Lexi wonders why God makes people like Ben. Why do we get sick? Why can't we all be healthy and not handicapped?*

—Susan, age 11

There's more wisdom in these letters than some adults manage to grasp in a lifetime. It's great to know that there are teenagers attempting to understand and to accept people with handicaps. After all, we're all God's children whether we're healthy or unhealthy, handicapped or free of disabilities. Our Creator loves each of us equally—why can't we do the same for each other?

I respect the person who can admit, "I never did like retarded people. Now I know better," or "I was scared in case someone saw me with them." That's honest. Honesty is the first step toward understanding.

Handicaps of any kind frighten us. We don't want to be handicapped ourselves, and we don't want it for our friends and family members. Even the thought of it is sometimes so alarming that we push it out of our minds. Even though we want to deny it, it could just as well have been you or me in that wheelchair, with that disability, with those problems. When a handicapped person is near, it's easier to walk by, pretending he's invisible, than it is to look him in the eye and smile. Yet ignoring people doesn't make them go away.

Some people tend to ridicule or make fun of things they

don't understand. It's childish and cruel. When you're tempted to laugh or make a hurtful remark about someone who is handicapped, just remember, it is *you* who will look bad, no one else.

When dealing with people with special needs, try to look past the disability to the person inside. That's what God does. "God does not see the same way people see. People look at the outside of a person, but the Lord looks at the heart" (1 Samuel 16:7).

That's good to know, isn't it? God loves you whether or not you have a zit on the end of your nose or a missing front tooth. Perfect bodies don't get you anywhere with God. What a relief! But what about your heart? Are you comfortable with how *that* looks? Is it full of pride and ridicule for others, or compassion and acceptance? Only you and God can know that.

## THIRTY – TWO

## "My Brother Died

● ● ● ● ● ● ● ● ●

*My brother died of an overdose of unprescribed medicine.*

—Stephanie, age 10

When something awful happens in your family, it sometimes feels like there is nowhere to turn, no one to talk to, nothing to be done. It's at times like these that the words David sang have special meaning: "The Lord is my rock, my protection, my Savior. My God is my rock. I can run to him for safety. He is my shield and my saving strength, my high tower" (Psalm 18:2).

I can't explain away death. Sometimes the only thing to do is to "run to Him for safety." After all, God promises to protect you through all kinds of troubles. "The Lord defends those who suffer. He protects them in times of trouble . . . He will not leave those who come to him" (Psalm 9:9–10). At a time like this, take Him up on His offer. He's there for you, willing to help. Let Him.

*Dear Judy,*

## When everything seems topsy-turvy and out of focus, God has an offer for you: Turn to Him.

*I read your first book and felt I knew the people in the book. My brother got killed the day after Christmas. He was five years old. My sister and I saw it. If he was still living he might be retarded, so when I read your book, I thought of my brother. After he died we had a tough time and were short on money, so we were sent to a different school. I only knew one person and there was a popular group I wanted to be in but I never was.*

—Jillian, age 14

When readers ask questions about death, I always find myself searching the Bible, looking for just the right words of comfort. It's important because death is an unalterable state. We can't change the fact that it's happened; we can only learn to deal with it.

The Psalms have particularly soothing verses, the kind that give assurance, comfort, and even hope.

"Give your worries to the Lord. He will take care of you. He will never let good people down" (Psalm 55:22).

"This God is our God forever and ever. He will guide us from now on" (Psalm 48:14).

God will guide you. He'll guide you through the hurt and confusion over the loss of your brother. He'll also lead you through the confusing maze of teenage popularity and acceptance. (But I'll cover more of that in Book #2 of *Dear Judy . . . .*)

Nothing is too big or too small for Him to be concerned about. Everything about you is important to Him. What great news that is!

# CONCLUSION

*You probably have a wonderful life—especially if you are writing about God.*

—Melissa, age 11

When I started this project, I had no idea how time-consuming, gut-wrenching, and emotionally draining it would be. I've discovered how deeply I care about you, the people who read my books. You are so important!

If I stress over and over again the importance of talking to your parents or another adult who can help you work through what troubles you, it is because I believe that is the best way to work through your problems. It's easy to pour your hearts out to me, but I'm far away. Sometimes getting feelings out on paper is enough. Other times, you need a person in your family, church, or school to help you work through what troubles you. Then the best gift I can get is a letter like this:

*I got your letter yesterday and I took your advice and talked to my parents. Everything is fine now with them. Thank you so-o-o much for helping me come to talk to my parents. I feel so much better now.*

*But, I better go. I just wanted to thank you.*

—Stacy, age 14

*Dear Judy,*

*When I have a big or small problem, I go to my parents or my pastor. They talk it over with me until I understand them. Then everything will be all right.*

—Natalie, age 12

*Talk to your parents. They love you!* Don't be afraid to share your thoughts, desires, wishes, and fears. They were your age once. Much of what you tell them will not shock or disappoint them. Your mom and dad have already traveled the road you are on now.

If you are in trouble and need help, here is a list of people you can talk to. They are there for you, but you must take the first step. No one will know you are frightened or hurting unless you tell them.

You can talk to:

- your mother
- your father
- a trusted relative, such as a grandparent
- your teacher
- the school counselor
- your pastor or priest

If the first person you approach cannot or does not help you, go to someone else. Not everyone will be capable of helping you, but you can find someone who is.

If you need help, be brave. Take that first step.

*Thank you, your book really helped me and my family work out all of our problems. Now we are doing fine. I hope I get to read another one of your books. I love your books; they really help me. I hope someday I can help teenagers work out their problems like you have helped me.*

—Leslie, age 14

*Thank you for your help and support even though you don't realize you are giving it to me.*

—Ginger, age 13

*I'm fourteen years old and am very fortunate. I am often told that I am very mature and have a good head on my shoulders. I have just finished reading* Broken Promises *and I think it's great that you know and understand how people feel and what is going on in the world today. I really enjoy reading your books. They give me encouragement to do what is right. I have two wonderful parents, and after reading this book it has made me realize that. Thank you for that. After reading this book I have a renewed faith in Christ, and I realize now that He does answer prayers and does care. My parents have raised me well and I never realized it or appreciated it before. Thanks again. You probably aren't used to getting letters like this, but after reading your books I feel that you really care.*

*P.S. Thank you for making me realize all that I have.*

—Mary, age 14

*What I really love about your books is that each one always leaves me thinking a number of things. I usually think about the huge problems of the characters, and then my so-called problems seem petty by comparison. I think about how good I have everything, especially two very wonderful parents whom I love and who love me. Then I think about Nicole Marlini in book #7. So many things that seem so bad to me, like what I'm going to do without that new pair of shoes, seems so ridiculous now. But, I guess making your readers think about these things is your job and let me tell you, you do an* excellent *job of it.*

—Cara, age 14

I guess it *is* my job to make my readers think. But they make *me* think even harder! Thank you for the letters. Thanks for making me think.

So then, what *is* it like at my house? It's sometimes funny there and sometimes serious. It's frustrating, rewarding, joyous, aggravating, irritating, hilarious, ridiculous, messy, neat, happy, sad, busy, noisy. Sound familiar? It's not perfect but it's nice. At our house, love is the glue that keeps us together.

The two letters that conclude this book will give you an

honest glimpse at my house. These letters are from my daughters to you, my readers. This was a brave request for me to make—especially since I told them they could say anything they wanted!

What's it like at my house? Let my girls tell you . . .

*Dear readers of Cedar River Daydreams,*

*When my mom told me that her editor would like me to write a note in her new book telling you what it's like at our house, I was excited. (Okay, so I was very excited— I'm only human!)*

*I thought to myself, "Here's my chance to get back at mom for all the times I've had to do laundry, clean the cat box, and pick up my room!*

*There was only one catch: I had to read the book before I wrote this letter.*

*I didn't realize what was in store for me.*

*Mom has always asked my opinion about things. Occasionally she asks me how I feel about the advice she's giving when she's answering her mail, but until I read this book, I never realized how many people come to her for answers to their questions.*

*What's it like at my house?*

*I guess I'm lucky. I'll never understand how it might be for a child who is not able to talk to his or her parents. My mom is always right there for me. If I have any complaint, it's that I wish she'd just let me pout once in a while. But that's not her style. If I'm down, she knows it and is all over me within seconds, asking what's wrong and if she can help. The only thing she tries to stay out of is the fights I have with my little sister. (I'm not sure she'll ever understand that relationship! After all, she never had a sister.)*

*Of course we have problems sometimes—everybody does—but somehow we work through them. (And usually we both end up happy.)*

*All in all, she's pretty neat. I think I'll keep her. I like it a lot at my house.*

*Adrienne Baer, age 16*

*My household is one-of-a-kind. Don't get me wrong—I'm very happy here and there are very few things I'd change if I had the opportunity.*

*There's no doubt that each of us is going in a hundred different directions at once. But what do you expect with two teenagers, a lawyer and an author in the house? Our family is not able to sit down for dinner together every night of the week, but on Sundays, after church, we all sit down to dinner and have a good talk.*

*Mom and Dad are great about coming to our basketball games, plays, concerts, or whatever we're involved in.*

*My sister and I are great friends and we hardly ever fight. But Mom, who was an only child, has a hard time understanding that we get along better than most sisters do.*

*I disagree with my parents on things like how old I should be to date and what my curfew should be, but we get through it!*

*My family is great and I wouldn't trade them for the world.*

*Jennifer Baer, age 13.*

# Cedar River Daydreams Series
## By Judy Baer

| Title | Topic |
| --- | --- |
| 1. New Girl in Town | Adjusting to new school |
| 2. Trouble with a Capital "T" | Popularity and peer pressure |
| 3. Jennifer's Secret | Dyslexia |
| 4. Journey to Nowhere | Rebellion |
| 5. Broken Promises | Teen pregnancy |
| 6. The Intruder | Jealousy (foster child) |
| 7. Silent Tears No More | Child abuse |
| 8. Fill My Empty Heart | Anorexia |
| 9. Yesterday's Dream | Death/Alzheimer's Disease |
| 10. Tomorrow's Promise | Alzheimer's Disease |
| 11. Something Old, Something New | Teen pregnancy/adoption |
| 12. Vanishing Star | Horror movies |
| 13. No Turning Back | Depression/suicide |
| 14. Second Chance | Overcoming adversity and disabilty |
| 15. Lost and Found | Teen alcoholism |
| 16. Unheard Voices | Disabilities/prejudice |
| 17. Lonely Girl | Befriending the homeless |
| 18. More Than Friends | Racial prejudice |

# RESOURCES

*The Christian Counselor's Pocket Guide*, Selwyn Hughes, Bethany House Publishers, Minneapolis, Minnesota. Copyright © 1980, 1985.

*The Everyday Bible*, New Century Version, Word Publishing. Copyright © 1987, 1988.

*Good Grief*, Granger & Westberg, Fortress Press, Philadelphia, Pennsylvania. Copyright © 1962.